Under the sea, buried deep in the ocean bed miles down, lie unbelievable deposits of the resources man has come to depend upon. Not only oil, uranium and other fuel sources, but actual treasure—pearls, precious unmined stones and metal elements, gold, silver—a whole untapped world of riches lying in wait for millenia.

There are other things that lie in wait also. And with the invasion by man of this last frontier, the things of the undersea depths united to defend their own.

As with any frontier, there were merchants, traders, miners and others who needed protection. So there was a Sub-Sea Academy—not only for protection, but for exploration of its own. Indeed, the Sub-Sea Fleet spearheaded the highly technological research, the building of undersea domes, the development of potentially mine-rich areas.

So it was the men of the Sub-Sea Academy who were the first to encounter the inhuman and near human creatures of the deep.

And don't miss

UNDERSEA CITY
UNDERSEA QUEST

Available from Ballantine Books

UNDERSEA FLEET

Frederik Pohl
and
Jack Williamson

BALLANTINE BOOKS • NEW YORK

An Intext Publisher

BALLANTINE BOOKS, INC.
101 Fifth Avenue, New York, N.Y. 10003

CONTENTS

1

The Raptures of the Depths

We marched aboard the gym ship at 0400.

It was long before dawn. The sea was a calm, black mirror, rolling slowly under the stars. Standing at sharp attention, out of the corner of my eye I could see the distant docks of the Sub-Sea Academy, a splash of light against the low dark line of Bermuda.

Cadet Captain Roger Fairfane rapped out: "Cadets! Ten-*hut!*"

We snapped to attention, the whole formation of us. The gym ship was a huge undersea raft, about as lively and graceful as an iceberg. The sub-sea tugs were nuzzling around it like busy little porpoises, hauling and pulling us around, getting us out to sea. We were still on the surface, standing roll-call formation on the deck of the gym ship, but already the raft was beginning to pitch and wallow in the swells of the open sea.

I was almost shivering, and it wasn't only the wind that came in from the far Atlantic reaches. It was tingling excitement. I was back at the Sub-Sea Academy! As we fell in I could sense the eagerness in Bob Eskow, beside me. Both of us had given up all hope of ever being on the cadet muster rolls again. And yet—here we were!

Bob whispered: "Jim, Jim! It gets you, doesn't it? I'm beginning to hope——"

He stopped abruptly, as the whole formation fell suddenly silent. But he didn't have to finish the sentence; I knew what he meant.

Bob and I—Jim Eden is my name, cadet at the Sub-

1

Sea Academy—had almost lost hope for a while. Out of the Academy, in disgrace—but we had fought our way back and we were full-fledged cadets again. A new year was beginning for us with the traditional qualifying skin-dive tests. And that was Bob's problem, for there was something in his makeup that he fought against but could not quite defeat, something that made skin-diving as difficult for him as, say, parachute-jumping would be for a man afraid of heights. It wasn't fear. It wasn't weakness. It was just a part of him.

"Count off!"

Captain Fairfane gave the order, and the whole long line of us roared out our roll-call. In the darkness—it was still far from dawn—I couldn't see the far end of the line, but I could see Cadet Captain Fairfane by the light of his flash-tipped baton. It was an inspiring sight, the rigid form of the captain, the braced ranks of cadets fading into the darkness, the dully gleaming deck of the gym ship, the white-tipped phosphorescence of the waves.

We were the men who would soon command the Sub-Sea Fleet!

Every one of us had worked hard to be where we were. That was why Bob Eskow, day after day, grimly went through the tough, man-killing schedule of tests and work and study. The deep sea is a drug—so my uncle Stewart Eden used to say, and he gave his whole life to it. Sometimes it's deadly bitter. But once you've tasted it, you can't live without it.

Captain Fairfane roared: "Crew commanders, *report!*"

"First crew, allpresentandaccountedforSIR!"

"Second crew, allpresentandaccountedforSIR!"

"Third crew, allpresentandaccountedforSIR!"

The cadet captain returned the salutes of the three crew commanders, whirled in a stiff about-face and saluted Lieutenant Blighman, our sea coach. "AllpresentandaccountedforSIR!" he rapped out.

Sea Coach Blighman returned the salute from where he stood in the lee of the bow superstructure. He strode swiftly forward, in the easy, loose-limbed gait of an old underseaman. He was a great, brown, rawboned man with the face of a starving shark. He was only a shadow to us in the ranks—the first pink-and-purple glow was barely

2

beginning to show on the horizon—but I could feel his hungry eyes roving over all of us. Coach Blighman was known through the whole Academy as a tough, exacting officer. He would spend hours, if necessary, to make sure every last cadet in his crews was drilled to perfection in every move he would have to make under the surface of the sea. His contempt for weaklings was a legend. And in Blighman's eyes, anyone who could not match his own records for depth and endurance was a weakling.

Fifteen years before, his records had been unsurpassed in all the world—which made it hard to match them! When he talked, we listened.

"At ease!" he barked at us. "Today you're going down for your depth qualification dives. I want every man on the raft to pass *the first time*. You're all in shape—the medics have told me that. You all know what you have to do—and I'll go through it again, one more time, in case any of you were deaf or asleep. So there's no excuse for not qualifying!

"Skin-diving is a big part of your Academy training. Every cadet has to qualify in one sub-sea sport in order to graduate; and you can't qualify for sports if you don't qualify to dive, right here and now this morning."

He stopped and looked us over. I could see his face now, shadowy but strongly marked. He said: "Maybe you think our sub-sea sports are rough. They are. We make them that way. What you learn in sports here at the Academy may help you save lives some day. Maybe it will be your own life you save!

"Sea sports are rough because the sea is rough. If you've ever seen the sea pound in through a hull leak, or a pressure-flawed city dome—well, then you know! If you haven't, take my word for it—the sea is *rough*.

"We have an enemy, gentlemen. The enemy's name is 'hydrostatic pressure.' Every minute we spend under the sea is with that enemy right beside us—always deadly, always waiting. You can't afford to make mistakes when you're two miles down! So if you've got any mistakes to make—if you're going to cave in under pressure—take my advice and do it here today. When you're in the Deeps, a mistake means somebody dies!

"Hydrostatic pressure! Never forget it. It amounts to

3

nearly half a pound on every square inch, for every foot you submerge. Figure it out for yourselves! At one mile down—and a mile's nothing, gentlemen, it's only the beginning of the Deeps!—that comes to more than a ton pressing on every square inch. Several *thousand* tons on the surface of a human body.

"No human being has ever endured that much punishment and lived to talk about it. You can't do it without a pressure suit, and the only suit that will take it is one made of edenite." Beside me, Bob Eskow nudged me. Edenite! My own uncle's great invention. I stood straighter than ever, listening, trying not to show the pride I felt.

There still was very little light, but Lieutenant Blighman's eyes missed nothing; he glanced sharply at Bob Eskow before he went on. "We're trying something new," he said. "Today you lubbers are going to help the whole fleet. We're reaching toward greater depths—not only with edenite suits, but in skin-diving. Not only are we constantly improving our equipment, the sea medics are trying to improve us!

"Today, for instance, part of your test will include trying out a new type of depth-adaptation injection. After we dive, you will all report to the surgeon for one of these shots. It is supposed to help you fight off tissue damage and narcosis—in simple words, it makes you stronger and smarter! Maybe it will work. I don't know. They tell me that it doesn't always work. Sometimes, in fact, it works the other way. . . .

"Narcosis! There's the danger of skin-diving, men! Get below a certain level, and we separate the real sea cows from the jellyfish. For down below fifty fathoms we come across what they call 'the rapture of the depths.'

"The rapture of the depths." He paused and stared at us seriously. "It's a form of madness, and it kills. I've known men to tear off their face masks down below. I've asked them why—the ones that lived through it—and they've said things like 'I wanted to give the mask to a fish!' Madness! And these shots may help you fight against it. Anyway, the sea medics say it will help some of you jellyfish. But some of you will find that the shots may

4

backfire—may even make you more sensitive instead of less!"

I heard Bob Eskow whisper glumly to himself, beside me: "That's me. That's my luck!"

I started to say something to encourage him, but Blighman's hungry eyes were roving toward our end of the formation; I took a brace.

He roared: "Listen—and keep alive! Some men can take pressure and some can not. We hope to separate you today, if there are any among you who can't take it. If you can't—watch for these warning signs. First, you may feel a severe headache. Second, you may see flashes of color. Third, you may have what the sea medics call 'auditory hallucinations'—bells ringing below the sea, that sort of thing.

"If you get any of these signs, *get back to the locks at once*. We'll haul you inside and the medics will pull you out of danger.

"But if you ignore these signals . . ."

He paused, with his cold eyes on Bob Eskow. Bob stood rigidly silent, but I could feel him tensing up.

"Remember," the coach went on, without finishing his last sentence, "remember, most of you can find berths on the commercial lines if you fail the grade here. We don't want any dead cadets."

He looked at his watch.

"That's about all. Captain Fairfane, dismiss your men!"

Cadet Captain Fairfane came front-and-center, barked out: "Break for breakfast! The ship dives in forty minutes, all crews will fall in for depth shots before putting on gear. Formation dis-MISSED!"

We ate standing and hurried up the ladder, Bob and I. Most of the others were still eating, but Bob and I weren't that much interested in chow. For one thing, the Academy was testing experimental depth rations with a faintly bilgy taste; for another, we both wanted to see the sun rise over the open sea.

It was still a long way off; the stars were still bright overhead, though the horizon was all edged with color now. We stood almost alone on the long, dark deck. We walked to the side of the ship and held the rail with both hands. At the fantail a tender was unloading two fathometers to measure and check our dives from the deck of the sub-sea raft itself. A working crew was hoisting one of them onto the deck; both of them would be installed there and used, manned by upperclassmen in edenite pressure suits to provide a graphic, permanent record of our qualifications.

The tender chugged away and the working crew began to bolt down the first of the fathometers. Bob and I turned and looked forward, down at the inky water.

He said suddenly: "You'll make it, Jim. You don't need any depth shots!"

"So will you."

He looked at me without speaking. Then he shook his head. "Thanks, Jim. I wish I believed you." He stared out across the water, his brow wrinkled. It was an old, old story, his fight to conquer the effects of skin-diving. "The raptures of the depths. It's a pretty name, Jim. But an ugly thing——" He stood up and grinned. "I'll lick it. I've got to!"

I didn't know what to say; fortunately, I didn't have to say anything. Another cadet came across the deck toward us. He spoke to us and stood beside me, looking out at the black mirror of the water and the stars that shimmered in it, colored by the rim of light around the sky. I didn't recognize him; a first-year man, obviously, but not from our own crew.

"How strange to see," he said, almost speaking to himself. "Is it always like this?"

Bob and I exchanged looks. A lubber, obviously—from some Indiana town, perhaps, getting his first real look at the sea. I said, a little condescendingly, "We're used to it. Is this your first experience with deep water?"

"Deep water?" He looked at me with surprise. Then he shook his head. "It isn't the water I'm talking about. It's the sky. You can see so far! And the stars, and the sun coming up. Are there always so many stars?"

Bob said curtly, "Usually there are a lot more. Haven't you ever seen stars before?"

The strange cadet shook his head. There was an odd hush of amazement in his voice. "Very seldom."

We both stared. Bob muttered, "Who are you?"

"Craken," he said. "David Craken." His dark eyes turned to me. "I know you. You're Jim Eden. Your uncle is Stewart Eden—the inventor of edenite."

I nodded, a little embarrassed by the eager awe in his voice. I was proud of my uncle's power-filmed edenite armor, that turns pressure back on itself so that men can reach the floors of the sea; but my uncle had taught me not to boast of it.

"My father used to know your uncle," David Craken told me quickly. "A long time ago. When they were both trying to solve the problem of the pressure of the Deep——"

He broke off suddenly. I stared at him, a little angrily. Was he trying to tell me that my uncle had had someone else's help in developing edenite? But it wasn't so; Stewart would never have hesitated to say so if it were true, and he had never mentioned another man.

I waited for the stranger to explain; but there was no explanation from him, only a sudden, startled gasp.

"What's the matter?" Bob Eskow demanded.

David Craken was staring out across the water. It was still smooth and as black as a pool of oil, touched with shimmers of color from the coming sun. But something had frightened him.

He pointed. I saw a faint swirl of light and a spreading patch of ripples, several hundred yards from the gym ship, out toward the open sea. Nothing more.

"What was that?" he gasped.

Bob Eskow chortled. "He saw something!" he told me. "I caught a glimpse of it myself—looked like a school of tuna. From the Bermuda Hatchery, I suppose." He grinned at the other cadet. "What did you think it was, a sea serpent?"

David Craken looked at us without expression.

"Why, yes," he said. "I thought it might be."

The way he said it! It was as though it were perfectly possible that there really had been a sea-serpent there, coming up off the banks below the Bermuda shallows. He spoke as though sea-serpents were real and familiar; as one of us might have said, "Why, yes, I thought it might be a shark."

Bob said harshly: "Cut out the kidding. You don't mean that. Or—if you did, how did you get into the Academy?"

David Craken glanced at him, then away. For a long moment he leaned forward across the rail, staring toward the spreading ripples. The phosphorescence was gone, and now there was nothing more to see.

He turned to us and shrugged. He smiled faintly. "Perhaps it was a tuna school. I hope so."

"I'm sure it was!" said Bob. "There aren't any sea-serpents at the Academy. That's a silly superstition!"

David Craken said, after a moment, "I'm not superstitious, Bob. But believe me, there are things under the sea that—— Well, things you might not believe."

"Son," Bob said sharply, "I don't need to be told about the sub-sea Deeps by any lubber! I've been there— haven't we, Jim?"

I nodded. Bob and I had been together through Thetis Dome in far, deep Marinia itself—the nation of underwater dome cities, lying deep beneath the dark Pacific, where both of us had fought and nearly lost against the Sperrys.

"The Sub-Sea Fleet has explored the oceans pretty thoroughly," Bob went on. "They haven't turned up any sea-serpents that I know of. Oh, there are strange things, I grant you—but man put those things there! There are tubeways running like subways under the ocean floor, and modern cities under the domes, and sub-sea prospectors roving over the ocean floor; and there aren't any sea-serpents, because they would have been seen! It's crazy superstition, and let me tell you, we don't believe in these superstitions here at the Academy."

"Perhaps you should," said David Craken.

"Wake up, boy!" cried Bob. "I'm telling you I've been in the Deeps—don't try to tell me about them. The only time either Jim or I ever heard the words 'sea-serpent' used, the whole time we were in Marinia, was by silly old yarn-spinners, trying to cadge drinks by telling lies. Where do you hear stories like that, Craken? Out in Iowa or Kansas, where you came from?"

"No," said David Craken. "That isn't where I came

from." He hesitated, looking at us queerly. "I—I was born in Marinia," he told us. "I've lived there all my life, nearly four miles down."

2

The Looters of the Sea

At the bow, the stubby little sub-sea tugs were puffing and straining at the cables, towing us at a slow and powerful nine knots toward the off-shore submarine slopes. It was full daybreak now, and the sky was a wash of color, the golden sun looming huge ahead of us, wreathed in the film of cloud at the horizon.

Bob Eskow said: "Marinia? You? You're from—— But what are you doing here?"

David Craken said gravely: "I was born near Kermadec Dome, in the South Pacific. I came to the Academy as an exchange student, you see. There are a few of us here— from Europe, from Asia, from South America. And even me, from Marinia."

"I know that. But——"

Craken said, with a flash of humor: "But you thought I was a lubber who'd never seen the sea. Well, the fact of the matter is that until two months ago I'd never seen anything else. I was born four miles down. That's why the sky and the sun and the stars seem—well, just as fantastic to me as sea serpents apparently are to you."

"Don't kid me!" Bob flashed. "The sea-bottoms have been well explored——"

"No." He looked at us almost imploringly, praying us to believe him. "They have not. There are a handful of cities, tied together with the tubes. There are explorers and prospectors in all the Deeps, an occasional deep-sea farm, a few miles away from the dome cities. But the floor of the sea, Bob, is *three times larger* than the whole Earth's dry-land area. Microsonar can find some things; visual observation can find a few more. But the rest of the sea-bottom is as scarcely populated and as unknown as Antarctica. . . ."

The warning klaxon sounded, and that was the end of our chat.

We raced across the deck toward the hatchways, even while the voice of sea coach Blighman rattled out of the loudspeaker:

"Clear the deck. Clear the deck. All cadets report for depth shots. We dive in ten minutes."

A dark, lean cadet joined us as we ran. "David," he called, "I lost you! We must go for the injections now!"

David said: "Meet my friend, Eladio Angel."

"Hi," Bob panted as we trotted along, and I nodded.

"Laddy's an exchange student, like me."

"From Marinia too?" I asked.

"No, no!" he cried, grinning. His teeth flashed very white. "From Peru. As far from Marinia as from here is my home. I——"

He stopped, staring toward the stern. We were queuing up at the hatchways, but something was happening. The working crew was yelling for Sea Coach Blighman.

We turned to look toward the stern. Lieutenant Blighman, his shark's eyes flashing, came boiling up out of the hatchway. We scattered out of his way as he raced toward the stern.

One of the fathometers was missing.

We could hear the excited cries of the working crew. They had been securing the first of the fathometers on deck, where it would provide a constant record of our dives. The second, still on the landing stage—was gone. Gone, when no one was looking. Nearly a hundred pounds of sea-tight casing and instruments; and it was gone.

We lined up to get our shots. Everyone was talking about the missing fathometer. "The working crew," Captain Fairfane said wisely. "They didn't lash it. A swell came along and——"

"There was no swell," said David Craken, almost to himself.

Fairfane glowered. "Ten-*hut!*" he barked. "There's too much noise in this line!"

We quieted down; but David Craken was right. There had been no swell, no way for the hundred-pound instru-

10

ment to fall over the side of the landing stage. It was just—gone. And it wasn't the first such incident, I remembered. The week before, a sub-sea dory, pneumatic powered, big enough for one man, had astonishingly disappeared from the recreation beach. Possibly, I thought excitedly, the two disappearances were connected! Someone in a sub-sea dory could have slipped up behind the gym ship, surfaced while the work crew was busy on deck, stolen the fathometer——

No. It was impossible. For one thing, the dory was not fast enough to catch even the waddling raft we were on; for another, the microsonars would have spotted it. Possibly a very fast skin-diver, lying in wait in our path and vectoring in to our course in the microsonar's blind spot, could have done it, but it was ridiculous to think of a skin-diver out that far on the Atlantic.

I thought for a moment of the fantastic remark David Craken had made—the sea serpent. . . .

But that was ridiculous.

The diving bells jangled, and the ungainly sub-sea raft tipped and wallowed down under the surface. Above us, the sub-sea tugs would be cruising about, one of the surface, one at our own level, to guard against wandering vessels and, if necessary, to render emergency rescue service.

We were ready for our qualifying dives.

The injections were a mild sting, a painful rubbing, and that was all. I didn't feel any different after they were over. Bob was wincing and trying not to show it; but he was cheerful enough as we raced from the sickbay to our diving-gear lockers.

The gym ship was throbbing underfoot as its little auxiliary engines, too small to make it a sea-going craft under its own power, took over the job of maintaining depth and station. I could smell the faint, sharp odor of the ship itself, now that the fresh air from the surface was cut off. I could almost see, in my mind's eye, the green waves foaming over the deck, and I could feel all the mystery and vastness of the sub-sea world we were entering.

Bob nudged me, grinning. He didn't have to speak; I knew what he was feeling. The sea!

Cadet Captain Fairfane broke in on us. I had seen him talking excitedly to Sea Coach Blighman, but I hadn't paid much attention; I thought it might have been about the missing fathometer.

But it was not. Fairfane came aggressively up to me, his good-looking face angry, his eyes blazing. "Eden! I want to talk to you."

"Yessir!" I rapped out.

"Never mind the sir. This is man-to-man."

I was surprised. Roger Fairfane and I were not particularly close friends. He had been quite friendly when Bob and I first came back to his class—then, without warning, cold. Bob's notion was that he was afraid I would go after his place as cadet captain, though that didn't seem likely; the post came as a result of class standings and athletic attainment, and Fairfane had an impressive record. But Bob didn't like him anyhow—perhaps because he thought Roger Fairfane had too much money. His father was with one of the huge sub-sea shipping companies—Roger never said exactly what his position was, but he made it sound important.

"What do you want, Roger?" I hung my sea jacket in the locker and turned to talk to him.

"Eden," he said sharply, "we're being cheated, you and I!"

"Cheated?" I stared at him.

"That's right! This Craken kid, he swims like a devil-fish! With him against us, we haven't got a chance."

I said: "Look, Roger, this isn't a race. It doesn't matter if David Craken can take the pressure a few fathoms deeper than you and——"

"It may not matter to you, but it matters to me. Listen, Eden, he isn't even an American! He's a transfer student from the sea. He knows more about sea pressure than the coach does! I want you to go to Lieutenant Blighman and protest. Tell him it isn't fair to have Craken swimming against us!"

"Why don't you protest yourself, if you feel that way?"

"Why, Jim!" Fairfane looked hurt. "It just wouldn't look right—me being cadet captain and all. Besides——"

Bob broke in: "Besides, you already did, and he turned you down. Right?"

Roger Fairfane scowled. "Maybe so. I didn't actually protest, I just—— Well, what's the difference? He'll listen to you, Eden. He might think I'm prejudiced."

"Aren't you?" Bob snapped.

"Yes, I am!" Roger Fairfane said angrily. "I'm a better man than he is, and better than his pet Peruvian too! That's why I resent being made to look like a fool when he's in his natural element. We're supposed to be diving against men, Eskow—not against fish!"

Bob was getting angry, I could see. I touched his arm to quiet him down. I said: "Sorry, Roger. I don't think I can help you."

"But you're Stewart Eden's nephew! Listen to me, Jim, if you go to Blighman he'll pay attention."

That was something Roger Fairfane hadn't learned, regardless of the grades he got in his studies. I was Stewart Eden's nephew—and that, along with five cents, would buy me a nickel's worth of candy bars at the Academy. The Academy doesn't care who your uncle is; the Academy cares who *you* are and what *you* can do.

I said: "I've got to get my gear on. Sorry."

"You'll be sorry before you're through with Craken!" Roger Fairfane blazed. "There's something funny about him. He knows more about the Deeps than——"

He stopped short, glared at us, and turned away.

Bob and I looked at each other and shrugged. We didn't have time to talk by then, the other cadets were already falling in by crews, ready to go to the locks.

We hurried into our diving gear. It was simple enough—flippers for the feet, mouthpiece and goggles for the face, the portable lung on the back.

It was a late-issue electrolung, one of the new types that generates oxygen by the electrolysis of sea water. Dechlorinators remove the poison gases from the salt. It saves weight; it extends the range considerably—for water is eight-ninths oxygen by weight, and there is an endless supply, as long as the strontium atomic battery holds out to provide the electric current.

But Bob put his on reluctantly. I knew why. As the old early lung divers had found, pure oxygen was chancy; for those who were prone to experience "the raptures of the

13

depths," oxygen in too great strength seemed to bring on seizures earlier and more violently than ordinary air.

Perhaps the injections would help. . . .

We filed into the lock in squads of twenty men, our fins slapping the deck. We were issued tight thermo-suits there —first proof that this was no ordinary skin-diving expedition; we would be going deep enough so that the water would be remorselessly cold as well as crushingly heavy above us.

We sat on the wet benches around the rim of the low, gloomy dome of the lock and Coach Blighman gave us our final briefing:

"Each of you has a number. When we flood the lock and open the sea door, you are to swim to the bow superstructure, find your number, punch the button under it. The light over your number will go out, proving that you have completed the test. Then swim back here and come into the lock.

"That's all there is to it. There's a guide line in case any of you are tempted to get lost. If you stick to the guide line, you can't get lost. If you don't——"

He stared around at us, his shark's eyes cold as the sea.

"If you don't," he rasped, "you'll put the sub-sea service to the expense of a search party for you—or for your body."

His eyes roved over us, waiting.

No one said anything. There wasn't really much chance of our being lost——

Or was there? One of the fathometers was missing. In the hookup as used on the gym ship, it was a part of the microsonar; without it, it might be very hard indeed to locate one dazed and wandering cadet, overcome by depth-narcosis. . . .

I resolved to keep an eye on Bob.

"Any questions?" Coach Blighman rapped out. There were no questions. Very well. Secure face-pieces! Open Sea Valves One and Three!"

We snapped our face-lenses and mouthpieces into place.

The cadet at the control panel saluted and twisted two plastic knobs. The sea poured in.

It came in two great jets of white water, foaming and crashing against the bulkhead. Blinding spray distorted our lenses, and the cold brine surged and pulled around our feet.

Coach Blighman had retreated to the command port, where he stood watching behind thick glass. As the lock filled we could hear his voice, sounding hollow and far away through the water, coming over the communicators: "Sea door open!"

Motors whined, and the sea door irised wide.

"Count and out!"

Bob Eskow was number-four man in our crew, just before me. I could hear him rap sharply four times on the bulkhead as he squeezed through the iris door.

I rapped five times and followed.

The raptures of the depths!

But they weren't dangerous, they were—being alive. All of the work and strain at the Academy, all of my life in fact, was pointed toward this. I was in the sea.

I took a breath and felt my body start to soar toward the surface, a hundred feet above; I exhaled, and my body dipped back toward the deck of the sub-sea raft. The electrolung chuckled and whispered behind my ear, measuring my breathing, supplying oxygen to keep me alive, a ten-story building's height below the waves and the sky. It was broad daylight above, but down here was only a pale greenish wash of light.

The deck of the gym ship—all gray steel and black shadow on the surface—was transformed into a Sinbad's cave, gray-green floor beneath us, sea-green, transparent walls to the sides. The guide line was a glowing, greenish snake stretched tautly out ahead of me, into the greenish glow of the water. There was no sense of being under-water, no feeling of being "wet"; I was flying.

I kicked and surged rapidly ahead of the guide line without touching it.

Bob was just ahead, swimming slowly, fingers almost touching the guide line. I dawdled impatiently behind him, while he doggedly swam to the bow superstructure and fumbled around the scoring rig. Our numbers were there, with the Troyon tubes glowing blue over the signal buttons. They stood out clearly in the wash of green light, but Bob seemed to be having trouble.

For a moment I thought of helping him—but there is an honor code at the Academy, strict and sharp: Each cadet does his own tasks, no one can coast on someone else's work. And then he found the button, and his number went out.

I followed him with growing concern, back along the guide line. He was finding it difficult to stay with the guide; twice I saw him clutch at it and pull himself along, as his swimming strokes became erratic.

And this at a hundred feet! The bare beginning of the qualifying dives!

What would happen at three hundred? At five?

Finally we were all back inside the lock, and the sea-pumps began their deep, purring hum. As soon as the water was down to our waists Coach Blighman rasped:

"Eden, Eskow! What were you jellyfish doing? You held up the whole crew!"

We stood dripping on the slippery duckboards, waiting for the tongue-lashing; but we were spared it. One of the other cadets cried out sharply and splashed to the floor. The sea-medics were there almost before the water was out of the lock. I grabbed him, holding his head out of the last of the water; they took him from me and quickly, roughly, stripped his face-piece and goggles away. His face was convulsed with pain; he was unconscious.

Sea Coach Blighman strode in, splashing and raging. Even before the sea medics had finished with him, he roared: "Ear plugs! Theres one in every crew! I've told you a hundred times—I've dinned it in to you, over and over—ear plugs are worse than useless below a fathom! Men, if you can't take the sea, don't try to hide behind ear plugs; all they'll do is let the pressure build up a little more—a very little more—and then they'll give in, and you'll have a burst eardrum, and you'll be out of the Academy! Just like Dorritt, here!"

It was too bad for Dorritt—but it saved us for the moment.

But only for the moment.

We weren't more than a yard out of the lock when Bob swayed and stumbled.

I caught his arm, trying to keep him on his feet at least until we were out of range of Coach Blighman's searching eyes. "Bob! Buck up, man! What's the matter?"

He looked at me with a strange, distant expression; and then without warning his eyes closed and he fell out of my grasp to the floor.

They let me come with him to the sick-bay; they even let me take one end of the stretcher.

He woke up as we set the stretcher down and turned to catch my eye. For a moment I thought he had lost his mind. "Jim? Jim? Can you hear me?"

"I can hear you, Bob. I——"

"You're so far away!" His eyes were glazed, staring at me. "Is that you, Jim? I can't see—— There's a green fog, and lightning flashes—— Jim, where are you?"

I said, trying to reassure him: "You're in the sick-bay, Bob. Lieutenant Saxon is right here. We'll fix you up——"

He closed his eyes as one of the sea medics jabbed him with a needle. It put him to sleep, almost at once. But before he went under I heard him whisper: "Narcosis. . . . I knew I'd never make it."

Lieutenant Saxon looked at me over his unconscious form. "Sorry, Eden," he said.

"You mean he's washed out, sir?"

He nodded. "Pressure sensitive. Sorry, but—— You'd better get back to your crew."

3

Dive for Record!

At seven hundred feet I swam out into blackness.

The powerful sub-sea floodlamps of the gym ship could no more than shadow the gloomy deck. There was no trace of light from the bright sun overhead, and only the dimmest corona, far distant, to mark the bow superstructure.

I felt—dizzy, almost sick.

Was it the pressure, I wondered, or was it my friend

Bob Eskow, back in the sick-bay? I had left him and gone back to the trials, but my thoughts stayed with him.

I tried to put him out of my mind, and stroked forward through the gloomy depths toward the faintly glowing bow superstructure, where my number had to be put out.

There were only seventeen of us left—the rest had completed a few dives and been disqualified by the sea-medics from going on, or had disqualified themselves. Or, like Bob Eskow, had cracked up.

Two were left from our original twenty-man crew—myself and one other—and fifteen from all the other crews combined. I recognized David Craken and the boy from Peru, Eladio; there was Cadet Captain Fairfane, glowering fiercely at the two foreign cadets; and a few more.

I left them behind and stroked out. There was no feeling of pressure on me, for the pressure inside my body was fully as great as the pressure without. The chuckling, whispering electrolung on my back supplied gas under pressure, filled my lungs and my bloodstream. Clever chemical filters sucked out every trace of chlorine, nitrogen and carbon-dioxide, so that there was no risk of being poisoned or of "the bends"—that joint-crippling sickness that came after pressure that had killed and maimed so many early divers.

A column of water seven hundred feet tall was squeezing me, but my own body was pushing back; I couldn't feel the pressure itself. But I felt ancient, weary, exhausted, without knowing why. I was drained of energy. Every stroke of the flippers on my feet, every movement of my arms, seemed to take all the strength in my body. Each time I completed a stroke it seemed utterly impossible that I would find the energy and strength necessary for another. I would be so much easier to let myself drift. . . .

But somehow I found the strength. And somehow, slowly, the greenish corona at the bow grew nearer. Its shape appeared; the fiercely radiant floodlights brightened and took form, and I began to be able to make out the rows of numbers.

Fumblingly I found the button and saw my own number flash and wink out. I turned and wearily, slowly, made my way back along the guide line, into the lock once more.

Nine hundred feet.

Only eleven of us had completed the seven-hundred-foot dive. And the sea medics, with their quick, sure tests, eliminated six out of the eleven. Eladio was one of those to go—Lt. Saxon's electro-stethoscope had detected the faint stirrings of a heart murmur; he curtly refused the Peruvian permission to go out again.

Five of us left—and two of the five showed unmistakable signs of collapse as soon as the water came pounding in; cadets in armor floundered out of the emergency locks and bore them away while the rest of us remained to feel the whining tingle of the motors opening the sea-gates and see the deeps open to us once more.

"The rest of us." There were only three now. Myself. And Cadet Captain Roger Fairfane—worn, strained, irritable, tense, but grimly determined. And David Craken, the cadet from Marinia.

There was not even a glow from the superstructure now. I dragged myself through the water, doggedly concentrating on the gleam of the guide line—how dully, how feebly it gleamed under the nine hundred feet!

It seemed as though I were trying to slide through jelly, for hours, making no progress. Suddenly I noticed something ahead—the faint, distant glimmer of lights (the bow floodlights—visible on the surface for a score of miles, but down here for only as many feet!) And outlined against them, some sort of weird, unrecognizable sea beings. . . .

There were two of them. I looked at them incuriously and then somehow I realized what they were: David Craken and Roger Fairfane. They had left the lock a moment before me, they had reached their goals and they were on their way back.

They passed me almost without a glance. I struggled onward wearily; by the time I had found my button and turned out my number, they were out of sight again.

I saw them again halfway back—or so I thought.

And then I realized that it could not be them.

Something was moving in the water near me. I looked

more closely, somehow summoning the strength to be curious.

Fish. Dozens of little fish, scurrying through the water, directly across my course along the guide line.

There is nothing strange about seeing fish in the Bermuda waters, not even at nine hundred feet. But these fish seemed—frightened. I stared wearily at them, resting one hand on the guide line while I thought about the strangeness of their being frightened. I glanced back toward where they had come from. . . .

I saw something, something I could not believe.

I could see—very faintly—the line of shadow against a deeper shadow that was the port rail of the gym ship. And traced in blacker shadow still, *something* hovered over that rail. There was almost no light, but it seemed to have a definite shape, and an unbelievable one.

It looked like—like a *head*. An enormous head, lifted out of the blackness below the deck. It was longer than a man, and it seemed to be looking at me through tiny, slitted eyes, yawning at me with a whole nightmare of teeth. . . .

I suppose I should have been terrified. But nine hundred feet down, with armor, I didn't have the strength to feel terror.

I hung there, one hand resting on the guide line, staring, not believing and yet not doubting.

And then it was gone—if it had ever been there.

I stared at the place where it had been, or where I had thought I had seen it, waiting for something to happen—for it to appear again, or for something to convince me that it had been only imagination.

Nothing happened.

I don't know how long I waited there. Then, slowly, I remembered. I was not supposed to stay there. I was supposed to be doing something. I had a definite goal. I was on my way back to the lock——

Painfully I forced myself into motion again.

That brightly gleaming line seemed a million miles long. I kept close to it, swimming as hard as I could, until the stern lights took form and the dome of the lock itself bulged out of the dark.

I dragged myself inside the sea-gate and looked back.

There was nothing there.

The sea-gates moaned and whined and closed, and the pumps forced the water out.

I don't know what the other two had seen—nothing, I suppose—but they looked as beaten, as exhausted as I did, when the last of the water was gone and Coach Blighman came swinging in from the escape hatch.

He was grinning, and when he spoke his voice resounded like thunder in the little room.

"Congratulations, men!" he boomed. "You're real sea-cows, you've proved that! The three of you have qualified at nine hundred feet—*nine hundred feet!*—and that's a record! In all the years I've been sea coach at the Academy, there haven't been half a dozen cadets to make the grade this far down—and now there are three of you in one class!"

I was beginning to catch my breath. I said: "Coach. Lieutenant Blighman, I——"

"Just a minute, Eden," he said sharply. "Before you say anything, I want to ask you all something." I wasn't sure what I had been going to say—something about the thing I had seen, or thought I had seen, I suppose. But in the brightly lightly little room, with Blighman talking about records, it seemed so utterly remote, that less and less could I believe that I actually had seen it.

Blighman was saying: "You've all qualified, no question about that. But Lieutenant Saxon has asked if any of you are willing to try another dive two hundred feet farther down. It's a strictly volunteer operation—no objections if any of you don't want to do it. But he has hopes that his new injections are going to make it possible to establish deeper and deeper records; and he would like to try a little more. What do you say, men?"

He looked us over, the shark's eyes glowing. He stopped at me. "Eden? Are you all right? You look like you might be getting some kind of reaction."

"I—I think perhaps I am, sir." I hesitated, trying to think of a way to tell him just what that reaction was. But—a giant serpentine head! How could I tell him that?

He didn't give me a chance. He barked: "All right, Eden, that lets you out. Don't argue with me. You've

21

made a splendid showing already—no sense going on unless you're *sure* you can take it. Craken?"

David said, almost too quietly to hear, "Yes, sir. I'm ready."

I remembered, looking at him, what he had said about sea serpents, just a short time before while we were still on the surface. And what I had said to him! For a moment I was tempted to warn him that his sea serpent was really there——

But probably it was only an effect of pressure and the injection, anyhow. There were no sea serpents! Everyone knew that. . . .

"Fairfane?"

Roger Fairfane said, with an effort: "I'm okay. Let's dive."

Sea Coach Blighman looked at him thoughtfully for a moment. Then he shrugged. I could read his mind as clearly as though he had spoken. Fairfane didn't look too well, that was sure—but, Blighman had decided, if there was anything wrong the sea medics would spot it, and if there wasn't, it didn't matter how the Cadet Captain looked.

The sea medics trotted in, made their quick checks, and reported both David and Roger in shape to go on.

Then Blighman curtly ordered the sea medics and me out of the lock. As I left I saw Roger Fairfane turn to glare at David, and I heard him mutter something.

It sounded like: "You'll never make a jellyfish out of me!"

Eleven hundred feet.

Coach Blighman let me come with him into the control room to watch Fairfane and David Craken swim their eleven-hundred-foot test.

The ship's motors rumbled and sang, bringing us down another two hundred feet, trimming the ballast tanks. It was important that the ship be kept dead still in the water—if it had been moving when any of us were swimming our trials, we would have been swept away by the motion of the water. The diving vanes fore and aft were useless for that reason; the trim of the ship depended only on the tanks.

Finally it was adjusted, and the lock was flooded.

I could see the sea-gates iris open—the round portals spinning wide like the opening of a camera lens. David and Roger came slowly out of the lock.

The thick lenses in the observation port made them look distorted and small. They swam painfully away into the gloom, queer little frogs, slower and more clumsy than the fish.

As soon as they were out of sight I began to feel guilty.

Crazy or not, I should have warned them of what I thought I saw. I waited, and they didn't come back—only seconds had passed, after all.

I began to squirm.

Hesitantly I said, "Sir."

Blighman paid no attention to me.

I blurted out: "Coach Blighman! That reaction—I didn't tell you, but what I thought I saw was——"

"There they are!" he cried. He hadn't heard a word I was saying. "There they come—both of them! They've made it!"

I looked, and I saw them too—the pair of them, coming slowly, limping, out of the dark. They kicked sluggishly toward us and it seemed to me that Roger Fairfane was in trouble.

Both of them moved slowly; but Fairfane looked weak, strained, erratic.

David Craken was swimming close alongside him and just above, keeping watch on him. They swam into the lock above us and I heard the doors whine shut.

It was over. I was glad I hadn't said anything about sea serpents. They had returned safely, the tests were at an end, and now we could go back to our life at the Academy.

Or so I thought. . . .

The coach splashed in before all the water was out, and I was at his heels. Roger Fairfane was sprawled on the bench, exhausted; David Craken was looking at him anxiously.

Blighman said exultantly: "Fine swimming, men! You're setting new records." He looked sharply at Roger. "Any reactions?"

Roger Fairfane blinked at him glassily. "I—I'm okay," he said.

"You, Craken?"

"I'm perfectly well, sir," said David. "I tried to explain to Lieutenant Saxon that I didn't need the shots at all. I am not sensitive to pressure."

Blighman looked at them, speculating. He said: "Do you feel fit for another dive?"

I couldn't help it. I burst in: "Sir, they've gone two hundred feet farther down already than the regulations——"

"Eden!" The voice was a whiplash. "I am in command of these tests! It's up to me to decide what the regulations say."

"Yes, sir. But——"

"Eden!"

"Yes, sir."

He stared at me for a moment with the cold shark's eyes, then he turned back to Roger and David. "Well?" he asked.

Roger Fairfane looked white and worn, but he managed to get the strength to scowl—not at Coach Blighman, but at David. He said: "I'm ready, Coach. I'll show him who's a jellyfish!"

David spoke up, his voice concerned. "Roger, listen. I don't think you ought to try it. You had a tough time making it back to the lock at eleven hundred feet. At thirteen hundred——"

"Coach!" cried Roger. "Get him off me, will you? He's trying to talk me out of a record because he can't swim me out of it!"

"No, please!" said David. "If the record is so important, I'll stop too. We'll leave it a tie. But it isn't safe for you, Roger. Can't you see that? It's different for me. I was *born* four miles down; pressure isn't important to me."

"I want to go through with it," said Roger doggedly.

And that was the way it was. Coach Blighman made the sea medics double-check both of them this time. Both came up with clear records—no physical reactions at all. Were there mental reactions?—the narcosis of the depths?

There was no way to tell, for anyone except David and Roger themselves. And both of them denied it.

The process of descending and trimming ship again seemed to take forever.

Thirteen hundred feet!

We were a quarter of a mile down now. On every square inch of the sturdy edenite hull of our sea-raft a force of more than five hundred pounds were pressing.

And that same force would be squeezing the weak, human flesh of David and Roger as soon as they began their test.

I heard the sea-gates whine open.

David came out—slowly, but sure of himself. After a moment Roger came into sight behind him. They both headed down along the guide line toward the invisible bow superstructure.

But Roger was in trouble.

I saw him veer away from the guide line, toward the starboard rail. He caught himself, jerked convulsively back, then seemed just to drift for a moment. His arms and legs were moving but without co-ordination.

"He's reacting!" Sea Coach Blighman said sharply. "I was afraid of that! But the tests were all right——"

Behind me the voice of Lieutenant Saxon said crisply: "Call him back!" I hadn't even seen Saxon come into the control room but I was glad for his presence then.

Blighman nodded abruptly. "You are right. Keep an eye on him——I'll try to reach him."

He trotted over to the deep-sea loud-hailer that would send a concentrated cone of vibrations through the water. Near the surface it could be heard by men in skin-diving outfits. But this far down——

Evidently it wasn't penetrating the enormous pressures of the depths. Perhaps the diaphragm couldn't even vibrate, with five hundred pounds squeezing at every inch of it. But whatever the cause, Roger didn't come back. He jerked convulsively and began to swim—steadily, slowly, evenly.

And in the wrong direction.

He was headed straight for the port rail and the depths beyond.

"Emergency crew! Emergency crew!" bellowed Blighman, and cadets in edenite depth armor clanked cumbersomely toward the emergency hatches.

But David Craken turned, looked for Roger, found him—and came back. He swam to overtake him, caught him still within sight of our observation ports.

He seemed to be having difficulties; it looked as though Roger was struggling, but it was hard to see clearly.

But whatever the struggle, David won. They came back, David partly towing Captain Roger Fairfane, into the lock.

Once more we had to wait for the pumps.

When we got inside the gloomy lock, Roger was lying on the wet bench with his goggles off, the mouthpiece hissing away as it hung from his shoulder harness. He looked pale as death; his eyes were bloodshot and glazed.

"Fairfane, are you all right?" rapped the coach.

Roger Fairfane took a deep breath. He said, choking, "He—he slugged me! That jellyfish slugged me!"

David Craken blazed: "Sir, that's not true! Roger was obviously in difficulty, so I——"

"Never mind, Cracken," snapped Blighman. "I saw what was happening out there. You may have saved his life. In any case, that's the end of the tests. Get out of your gear, all of you."

Roger Fairfane hauled himself erect. "Lieutenant Blighman," he said formally, controlling his rage, "I protest this! I was attacked by Cadet Craken because he was afraid I'd beat him. I intend to take this up with the cadet court and——"

"Report to sick-bay!" cried Blighman. "Whether you know it or not, you're reacting to Saxon's serum or to pressure! Don't let me hear any more from you now!"

He left. Grudgingly and angrily, but he left.

And once again I thought that was an end to the tests.

And once again I was wrong.

For David Craken, looking weary but determined, said: "Sir, I request permission to complete the thirteen-hundred-foot test."

"What?" demanded Blighman, for once off balance.

"I request permission to complete the test, sir," David repeated doggedly. "I didn't strike Captain Fairfane. It would be fairly simple for me to complete the test. And I request permission to demonstrate it."

Blighman hesitated, scowling. "Craken, you're at thirteen hundred feet. That isn't any child's game out there."

"I know, sir. I'm a native of Marinia. I've had experience with pressure before."

Blighman looked him over thoughtfully. Then he nodded abruptly.

"Very well, Craken. Lieutenant Saxon says these tests are important to help establish his serum. I suppose that justifies it. You may complete your dive."

We went down once more to the control chamber.

The sea-gates opened above us, and I watched David come swimming out into the cold blackness of the water at a quarter of a mile's depth.

He looked as slow and clumsy as human swimmers always do under the water, but he stroked regularly, evenly, down the glowing guide line until he was out of sight.

We waited for him to return.

We waited for seconds. Then minutes.

He swam down the guide line past the threshold of invisibility. And he never came back.

4

"The Tides Don't Wait!"

The next day it all seemed like a bad dream.

There was no time for dreaming, though. It was Academy Day, and the big inspection and review had us all on the hop.

Over the sea-coral portals of the Administration Building, etched in silver, was the motto of the Academy: *The Tides Don't Wait!* The tides don't wait for anything—not for a lost shipmate, not for tragedy, not for any human affair. David Craken was gone, but the Academy went on.

We fell in, in full-dress sea-scarlet uniforms, on the blindingly white crushed coral of the Ramp. Overhead the bright Bermuda sun shone fiercely out of a sky full of fleecy clouds. The cadet officers snapped their orders, the long files and crews went through the manual of arms and wheeled off in parade formation. As we passed David Craken's crew I risked a glance. There was not even a gap to mark where he should have been. I saw Eladio Angel, his face strained but expressionless as he stood at stiff attention, waiting for the order to march off; David would have been marching beside him.

But David was—well, the wording of the official notice on our bulletin board was "lost and presumed drowned."

The band blared into the sub-sea anthem as we wheeled left off the Ramp, boxed the Quadrangle and halted by squads in the center of the square, facing the inspection platform in front of the Ad Building. The sun was murderously hot, though it was not yet noon; but not a man of our class wavered. We stood there while the upperclassmen marched crisply through in their turn; we stood there through the brief address by the Commandant to remind us of the sacredness of the day. We stood there through the exacting man-by-man inspection of the Commandant and his officers, as they strolled down the lines, checking weapons, eagle-eyed for a smudged tunic or tarnished button.

Then it was over and we marched off again by crews, to be dismissed at the end of the Ramp. Bob Eskow and I fell out and began to trot for our quarters—we had just twenty minutes before we were due to fall out again in undress whites for our first class of the day.

We were stopped by a cadet from the Guards crews. "Eden?" he snapped. "Eskow?"

That's right," I told him.

"Report to the Commandant's office, both of you. On the double."

We stared at each other. The Commandant! But we had done nothing to justify being reprimanded. . . .

"*On the double*, lubbers!" the Guard cadet barked. "What are you waiting for? The tides don't wait!"

They called me first. I left Bob sitting at ramrod attention in the Commandant's outer office, opened the door to the private room, took a deep breath and entered. My hat was properly under my arm, my uniform was as nearly perfect as I could make it; at least, I thought, if the Commandant had to call me in, in was nice of him to make it right after a full-dress inspection! I saluted and said, with all the snap I could give it: "Sir, Cadet Eden, James, reporting to the Commandant as ordered!"

The Commandant, still in his own dress uniform, mopped at his thick neck with a sea-scarlet handkerchief and looked me over appraisingly.

"All right, Eden," he said after a moment. "Stand at ease."

He got up and walked wearily to a private door of his office. "Come in, Lieutenant," he called.

Sea Coach Blighman marched stiffly into the room. The Commandant stood for a moment at the window, looking somberly out at the bright, white beaches and the blue sea beyond. Without turning, he said:

"Eden, we lost a shipmate of yours yesterday in the diving tests. His name was David Craken. I understand you knew him."

"Yes, sir. Not very well. I only met him a short time before the dive, sir."

He turned and looked at me thoughtfully. "But you did know him, Eden. And I'll tell you something you may not know. You are one of the very few cadets in the Academy who can say that. His roommate—Cadet Angel. You. And just about nobody else. It seems that Cadet Craken, whatever his other traits, did not go in for making friends."

I remained silent. When the Old Man wanted me to say something, he would let me know, I was sure of that.

He looked at me for a moment longer, his solid, ruddy face serious. Then he said: "Lieutenant Blighman, have you anything to add to your report on Cadet Craken?"

"No, sir," rasped Coach Blighman. "As I told you, as soon as Cadet Craken failed to return in a reasonable time I alerted the bridge and requested a microsonar search. They reported that the microsonar was not fully operative, and immediately beamed the escort tugs, asking them to conduct a search. It took a few minutes for the tugs to reach us, and by the time they did they could find no trace of Cadet Craken."

I thought of David Craken, out alone in the icy, dark sea, under the squeeze of thirteen hundred feet of water. It was no wonder the tugs had been unable to locate him. A man's body is a tiny thing in the immensity of the sea.

The Commandant said: "What about the microsonar? What was the trouble with it?"

Blighman scowled. "Well, sir," said, "I—I don't know that it makes sense."

"I'll decide that," the Commandant said with an edge to his voice.

"Yes, sir." Blighman was clearly unhappy; he frowned at me. "In the first place, sir, one of the fathometer rigs was apparently lost from the deck of the gym ship before the dive. Since the microsonar had been adapted to use two fathometers to make an official diving record, that may have affected its efficiency. At any rate, the search room reported a—a ghost image. They had stripped down the sonar to find the trouble when Craken was lost."

"A ghost image," repeated the Commandant. He looked at me. "Tell Cadet Eden what that image was supposed to be, Lieutenant."

"Well—— The sonar crew thought it, well, looked something like a sea serpent."

The Commandant let the words hang there for a moment.

"A sea serpent," he repeated. "Cadet Eden, the Lieutenant tells me that you said something about a sea serpent."

I said stiffly, "Yes sir. I—I thought I saw something at eleven hundred feet. But it could have been anything, sir. It could have been a fish, or just my imagination— narcosis or something like that, sir. But——"

"But you used the term 'sea serpent,' did you not?"

I swallowed. "Yes, sir."

"I see," The Commandant sat down at his desk again and looked at his hands. "Cadet Eden," he said, "I've investigated the disappearance of Cadet Craken as thoroughly as I could. There are several aspects to it on which I have not fully made up my mind. In the first place, there is the loss of the fathometer. True, it was not secured, for which I have already disciplined the working crew responsible, and it may merely have slipped over the side. But there have been several such incidents. And in this case it may have cost us the life of a cadet.

"Second, there is the suggestion that a sea serpent may somehow be involved. I must say, Eden, that I am instinctively inclined to think all sea serpents come out of bottles. I've spent forty-six years in the sub-sea service and I've been in some funny places; but I've never seen a sea serpent. The microsonar crew isn't very sure of what they saw—if they saw anything at all—and besides we know that the equipment was operating badly because of the loss of the fathometer. That puts it up to you. Can you say positively that you saw a sea serpent?"

I thought rapidly, but there was only one conclusion. "No, sir. It may have been a reaction, either from the depth serum or from narcosis."

The Commandant nodded. "I thought so. So there remains only point three.

"Cadet Eden, I have already interviewed Cadet Captain Roger Fairfane. He reports that there was a serious disagreement between Cadet Craken and himself, and it is his opinion after due reflection that Cadet Craken may have been in an unstable mental state at the time of his final dive. In other words, Eden, Captain Fairfane suggests that Craken may deliberately have gone over the side and straight down, in order to commit suicide."

I completely forgot Academy discipline.

"Sir!" I blazed. "Sir, that's ridiculous! Fairfane's crazy if he thinks David would have killed himself! Why, in the first place, the whole fight between them was Fairfane's own doing—and besides David had absolutely no reason to do anything of the sort! He might have been a little— well, odd, sir, keeping to himself and so on, but I'll swear he wasn't the kind to commit suicide. Why, he was——"

I stopped, suddenly remembering who and where I was. Lieutenant Blighman was frowning fiercely at me, and even the Commandant was looking at me with narrowed eyes.

"Sorry, sir," I said. "But—no, sir, it's impossible. Cadet Craken couldn't have killed himself."

The Commandant took a moment to think it over. Then he said:

"All right, Cadet Eden. If it is of any interest to you, I may say that your estimate agrees with Lieutenant Blighman's. In his opinion Cadet Craken—like yourself, I might mention—is, or was, one of the most promising cadets in the Academy. Dismissed!"

I saluted, turned and left—but not before I caught a glimpse of Lieutenant Blighman, looking embarrassed. The old shark! I thought to myself, wonderingly. Evidently behind those fierce and hungry eyes there was a human being, after all.

Because it was Academy Day, there was only one class that afternoon, and Eladio Angel was in it with me. Since Bob didn't return from the Commandant's office before it was over, Laddy—so David Craken had called him—and I left together.

We walked toward his quarters, comparing notes on what the Commandant had said to us. It had been about the same for both of us—Laddy was as furious as I at Fairfane's suggestion that David had committed suicide. "That squid Fairfane, Jeem," he said, "he hates greatly. David is beyond question a better diver, no? So when he is lost, the squid must destroy his name." He looked at me searchingly for a moment. "And also," he added, "I do not think David ees dead."

I stopped and stared at him. "But——"

Eladio Angel held up his hand to interrupt me. "No, no," he begged, "do not tell me he is lost. For I know this, Jeem, and also I know David. I cannot say why I think it, but think it I do." He shrugged with a small smile. "But he ees declared missing and presumed to be drowned, that is true. And so no matter what Eladio thinks, Eladio must abide by what the Academy says. So I am packing his things now, Jeem, to send them back to his father near Kermadec Dome." He hesitated, then asked: "Would you—would you care to see something, Jeem?"

I said, "Well, thanks. But it doesn't seem right to pry."

"No, no! No prying, Jeem. It is only something that

32

you might like to see, Jeem. Nothing personal. A—a thing that David made. It is not only not private, it is hanging on the wall for all to see. Perhaps you should see it before I take it down."

Well, why not? Although I hadn't known David Craken well, I thought of him as a friend, and I was curious to see what Laddy Angel was talking about. We went to the room he had shared with David, and I saw it at once.

The spot over the head of a cadet's bed is his own, to do with as he will. Half the cadets in the Academy have photos of their girl friends hanging there, most of the other half have their mothers' pictures, or photos of sub-sea vessels, or once in a while a signed portrait of some famous submariner or athlete.

Over David Craken's bed hung a small, unframed water color.

He had painted it himself; it was signed "DC" in the lower right-hand corner. And it showed——

It was a sub-sea scene. A great armored sub-sea creature was bursting out of a tangled forest of undersea plants.

There was very little about the scene that was familiar, or even believable. The vegetation was strange to me—vast thick leaves, somehow looking luminous against the dark water. The armored thing itself was just as strange, with a very long neck, wicked fanged flippers——

But with the same head I had seen over the side of the gym ship—*if* I had seen anything—eleven hundred feet down.

And there was something that was odder still:

When I looked more closely at the picture, I saw that the monster was not alone. Seated on its back, jabbing at it with a long goad like a mahout on an elephant, was a human figure.

For a moment I had been shocked into believing fantastic things. Sea serpents!

But the human figure put a stop to it. I might have believed in the existence of sea serpents. I might have thought that his picture was some sort of corroboration of what I had thought I had seen and what the sonarmen thought they had picked up and what David had talked about.

33

But the man on the monster's back—that made it pure fantasy, the whole thing, just something that a youth from Marinia had painted to idle away some time.

I thanked Eladio for letting me see the picture and left.

Bob still had not returned from the Commandant's office.

I went to chow and returned; still no Bob. I began to worry. I had thought it was only to ask him for his report on David's loss that he had been called in; but surely it couldn't have taken that long. I began to fear that it was something worse. Lieutenant Blighman was there with the Commandant; could it be that the sea coach had called Bob in in order to disqualify him? Certainly he was now a borderline case. All of us were required to qualify in one sub-sea sport a year to retain our status in the Academy, and Bob had now washed out in three of the four possibles. The marathon sub-sea swim was still to come, and he would not usually wash out unless he failed in that one too—but what other explanation could there be?

There was no point in sitting around worrying. I had got an address from Eladio of David Craken's father in Marinia. I sat down and began to write him a letter.

The address was:

> Mr. J. Craken
> Care of Morgan Wensley, Esq.
> Kermadec Dome
> Marinia

There wasn't much I could say, but I was determined to say something. Of course, the Academy would notify the elder Mr. Craken; but I wanted to say something beyond the bare, official radiogram. But on the other hand, it would be foolish to stir up worry and questions by saying anything about sea serpents, or about the disagreement with Cadet Captain Roger Fairfane. . . .

In the end, I merely wrote that, though I hadn't known David long, I felt a deep sense of loss; that he was a brave and skillful swimmer; and that if there was anything I could do, his father had only to ask me.

As I was sealing the letter Bob came in.

He looked worn but—not worried, exactly; excited was

34

a better word. I pounced on him with questions. What had happened? Had he been there all this time over David's disappearance? Were there any developments?

He laughed, and I felt relieved. "Jim, you worry too much. No, there aren't any developments. They asked me about David, all right. I just said I didn't know anything, which was perfectly true."

"And that took you all this time?"

His smile vanished. He looked suddenly—excited again. But he shook his head. "No, Jim," he said, "that isn't what took me all this time."

And that was all he said.

I didn't ask him any more questions. Evidently, I thought, Coach Blighman had given him a hard time after all. No doubt he had been put through a rough session, with both the Coach and the Commandant hammering at him, telling him that his record of sub-sea qualification was miserably unsatisfactory, reminding him that if he didn't qualify in the one remaining sub-sea sport activity of the year he would wash out. It was no wonder, I thought, that he didn't want to talk about it; it must have been an unpleasant experience.

The more I thought of it, the more sure I got that that was it.

And the more sure I got, the wronger I—much later—turned out to be.

5

Visitor from the Sea

That was in October.

Weeks passed. I got a curt note on the letterhead of Morgan Wensley, from Kermadec Dome. My letter had been received. It would be forwarded to Mr. Craken. The letter was signed by Morgan Wensley.

Not a word about the disappearance of David Craken. This Morgan Wensley, whoever he was, showed no regret and no interest.

As far as he was concerned, and as far as the Academy was concerned, David Craken might never have existed. David's name was stricken from the rolls as "lost." Laddy Angel and I met a few times and talked about him—but what was there to say, after all? And, since we weren't in the same crew, weren't even quartered in the same building, the times we met were fewer and fewer.

I almost began to forget David myself—for a while.

To tell the truth, none of us had much time for brooding over the past. Classes, formations, inspections, sports. We were kept busy, minute by minute, and whenever we had an hour's free time we spent it, Bob Eskow and I, down by the shallows, practicing skin-diving. Bob was fiercely determined that when the big marathon underwater swim came up after the holidays he would be in the best shape he could manage. "Maybe I'll wash out, Jim," he told me grimly, sitting and panting on the raft between dives. "But it won't be because I haven't done the best I can!" And he was off again with his goggles in place, stretching his breathing limit as far as it would go. I was hard put to keep up with him. At first he could stay down only a matter of seconds. Then a minute, a minute and a half. Then he was making two-minute dives, and two and a half. . . .

From earliest childhood I was a three-minute diver, but that was nearly the limit; and by Christmas holidays Bob was able to pace me second for second.

Without air supply, with only the oxygen in our lungs to keep us going, both of us were going down forty and fifty feet, staying down for as much as three and a half minutes. We worked out a whole elaborate system of trials. We checked out a pair of electrolungs and spent a whole precious Saturday afternoon underwater near the raft, marking distances and depths, setting ourselves goals and targets. Then every succeeding Saturday, in fair weather or foul, we were out there, sometimes in pounding rain and skies so gloomy that we couldn't see the underwater markers we had left.

But it paid off for Bob.

It showed on him in ways other than increased skill beneath the water. He began to lose weight, to grow leaner and wirier. When Lieutenant Saxon checked him over just before the Christmas holidays he gave Bob a sharp look. "You're the one who passed out in the diving tests?"

"Yes, sir."

"And now you want to kill yourself completely, is that it?" the sea medic blazed. "Look at your chart, man! You've lost twenty pounds! You're running on nerve and guts, nothing else. What have you been doing to yourself?"

Bob said mutinously: "Nothing, sir. I'm in good health."

"I'm the judge of that!" But in the end Saxon passed him, grumbling. Bob was wearing himself down to seabottom, but there is no law that says a cadet must pamper himself. And the grinding routine went on. Not only the Saturday-afternoon extra-duty swimming with me, but Bob developed a habit of stealing off by himself at the occasional odd hours between times—just after chapel, or during Visitors' Hour, or whenever else he could find a moment. I knew how worried he was that he might not pass the marathon-swim. I didn't question him about these extra times, for I was sure they were spent either in the gym or out doing roadwork to build up his wind.

Of course, I was utterly wrong.

Time passed—months of it. And at last it was spring.

We had almost forgotten David Craken—strange, sad boy from under the sea! It was April and then May, time for the marathon swim.

We boarded the gym ship again just after lunch. It was the first time Bob or I had been aboard her since David was lost. I caught Bob's eye on the spot where he and David and I had stood against the rail, looking back at the Bermuda shore. He saw me looking at him and smiled faintly. "Poor David," he said, and that was all.

That was all for him. For me, I was seeing something else at that rail—something large and reptilian, a huge, angular head that had loomed out of the depths.

I had seen it many times since—in dreams. But that first time, had *that* been a dream?

There was no time for dreaming now. No sooner were

we well clear of land than Cadet Captain Roger Fairfane called us to fall in in crews, and Sea Coach Blighman put us through an intensive workout, there on the deck of the sub-sea raft being towed through the Bermuda waves by the snub-nosed tugs. We had fifteen minutes of that, then a ten-minute break.

Then we were all ordered below decks. The hatches were sealed, the gym ship trimmed for diving, the signal made to the tugs, and we went to ten fathoms, to continue our voyage underwater. It was ten nautical miles to where we were going; at the nine-knot speed of the towed gym ship, a few minutes over an hour. Ten nautical miles, at 6,000 feet each. Sixty thousand feet. Nearly eleven and a half land miles.

And we would swim those miles back to base, maintaining our ten-fathom depth until we reached the shallows.

Halfway out, we were ordered into swimming gear, flippers, goggles, electrolung and thermo-suits. The suits would slow us down, but we had to have them. At ten fathoms—sixty feet—pressure is not the enemy. Cold is what is dangerous. Yes, cold! Even in Bermuda waters, even in late spring. The temperature of the human body is 98 degrees Fahrenheit and a bit; the temperature of sea water—even there and then—only in the seventies. Put a block of steel the size and temperature of the human body into the Bermuda sea, and in minutes it will cool to the temperature of the water around it. There is a difference between a block of steel and a human body, of course. The difference is this: It doesn't hurt a block of steel to be cooled to seventy degrees; but at that temperature the body cannot live.

What keeps swimmers alive? Why, the heat their bodies produce, of course; for the body is tenacious of its heat, and keeps pouring calories out to replace the loss. But add to the drain of heat-calories from the cooling of the water the drain of energy-calories of the muscles propelling the swimmer along, and in ten sea miles the body's outpouring of calories has robbed its reserves past the danger point.

The early surface swimmers—the conquerors of the English Channel, for example—tried to keep out the chill with heavy layers of grease covering every inch of the body but the eyes. Worse than useless! The grease actually helped to dissipate the heat. Oh, some of them made it, all the same. But how many others—even helped by frequent pauses in mid-Channel to drink hot beverages—failed?

There were a hundred and sixty-one of us on the gym ship. And it was the tradition of the Academy that *none* of us should fail.

As we climbed the ladders to the sea-lock I punched Bob's arm. "You'll make it!" I whispered.

He grinned at me, but the grin was worried. "I have to!" he said. And then we were in the lock.

The sea-gates irised open.

The gym ship, trimmed and motionless at ten fathoms, disgorged its hundred and sixty-one lungdivers by crews.

Silently, in the filtered green sunlight from above, we went through a five-minute underwater calisthenic warm-up. Then we heard the rumbling, wavering voice of Sea Coach Blighman on the hailer from the control deck. "Crew leaders, attention! At the signal, by crews, shove off!"

There was a ten-second pause, then the shrill, penetrating beep of the signal.

We were off.

Bob and I were in the last crew, commanded by Roger Fairfane. I had made up my mind to one thing: I would not leave Bob alone. Almost at once our regular formation broke up. I could see ten, twenty, perhaps thirty swimmers scattered about me in the water, looking like pale green ghosts stroking along in the space-eating swim the Academy taught us. I found Bob and clung close to him, keeping an eye on him.

He saw me, grinned—or so it seemed, with the goggles and mouthpiece hiding most of his face—and then concentrated his energies on the long swim before us.

The first mile. Cadet Captain Roger Fairfane came in close to us, waving angrily. We were well behind the others and he wanted us to catch up. I shook my head determinedly and pointed to Bob. Roger grimaced furiously, shot ahead, then returned. He stayed sullenly close all through the long swim. As crew officer, it was his duty to keep tabs on stragglers—and we were straggling.

The second mile. Bob kept right on plugging. We weren't making any speed, but he showed no signs of faltering.

The third mile. The cold was seeping in now; we were all beginning to feel the strain and weariness. All the others were well out of sight by now. Bob paused for a second in his regular, slow kick-and-stroke. He rolled over on his back, stretched—

And did a complete slow loop under water.

Roger and I shot toward him, worried. But he straightened out, grinned at us again—no mistake this time!—and made a victory signal with his hand.

For the first time I realized that the long months of training had paid off, and Bob was going to make it all the way.

We pulled ourselves out into the surf about a mile down the beach from the Academy compound. It was nearly dark by now; the rest of the swimmers must long since have returned.

Weary as we were, Bob and I clasped hands exultantly. Roger, impatiently standing in the shallows waiting for us, snarled something irritable and sharp, but we weren't listening. Bob had made it!

Roger opened the waterproof pouch at his waist and took out the flare pistol. He pointed it up and out to sea and fired the rocket that announced our safe arrival—necessary, so that the tally-officer would know we were not lost and hopeless, and so send out searching parties. "Come on," he growled. "We're halfway off the island and it's about chow time!"

Bob and I stripped off goggles and mouthpieces and drew deep breaths of the warm, fragrant air. We slid out of our thermo-suits and stood grinning at each other for a moment. "Come on!" Roger cried again. "What are you waiting for?"

We splashed toward him, still grinning. We could see the yellow lights shining in the big resort hotels beyond the Academy compound, and a glow of light in the sky over Hamilton. A full moon was well up on the horizon.

The scarlet all's-well flare went up from the Academy docks just then—proof that our signal had been the last; everyone had now completed the swim.

Roger yelled furiously: "Wake up, will you? Eskow! Get a move on. You held the whole crew up, you dumb jellyfish, and——"

He broke off suddenly, looking at the water between us.

A wave had washed something past us, up toward the high-water mark on the beach. Something that glowed, faint and blue.

It was a little metal cylinder, no larger than a sea-ration can. The wave broke and retreated, sucking the little cylinder back.

Bob bent down, curious even in his exhausted state, and picked it up.

We all saw it at once. The faint blue glow was the glimmer of edenite!

"Hey, Jim!" he cried. "Something armored! What in the world——?"

We stared at it. Armored with edenite! It had to be something from the deeps—edenite was for high-pressure diving, nothing else. I took it from his hand. It was heavy, but not so heavy that it couldn't float. The glow of the edenite was very pale, here in the atmosphere, but the tiny field-generators inside the cylinder must still be working—I could see the ripple of light shimmer across it as my breath made a pressure change on the cylinder.

And I saw a dark line, where two halves of it joined.

"Let's open it," I said. "It must unscrew—here, where the line goes around it."

Roger splashed toward us. "What have you got there?" he demanded, his swimming fins kicking spray and digging into the coral sand. "Let me see!"

Instinctively I handed it back to Bob. He hesitated, then held it toward Roger—but without letting go.

Roger grabbed at it. "Give it here!" he rasped. "I saw it first!"

"Now, wait a minute," Bob said quietly. "I felt it wash against my ankle before you ever saw it. You were too busy calling me a jellyfish to——"

41

"It's mine, I say!"

I broke in. "Before we worry too much about it, why don't we open it up and see what's inside?"

They both looked at me. Roger shrugged disdainfully. "Very well. But remember that I am your cadet officer. If its contents are of any importance, it will be my duty to take charge of them."

"Sure," said Bob, and handed the cylinder to me. I caught the ghost of a wink in his eye, though his expression was otherwise serious.

I gripped the ends of the thing and twisted. It unscrewed more easily than I had expected, and as soon as it began to turn the glimmer of the edenite armor flickered and died. The connection to the tiny generators within it had been broken.

The metal cap came off, and I shook the cylinder upside down over my hand.

The first thing that came out was a thick roll of paper. We looked at it and gasped—that paper was money! A great deal of it, by the feel, rolled up and held with a rubber band. Next came a document of some sort—perhaps a letter—rolled to fit in the cylinder. Tucked inside the letter was a small black velvet bag. I loosened the drawstrings of the bag and peered inside.

I couldn't help gasping.

"What is it?" Roger rapped impatiently.

I shook my head wordlessly and poured the contents of the bag out into the palm of my hand.

There were thirteen enormous pearls, glimmering like milky edenite in the yellow moonlight.

Thirteen pearls!

They looked as huge and as bright as the moon itself. They were all perfect, all exactly the same size. They seemed to shine with a light of their own in my hand.

"Pearls!" gasped Roger. "Tonga pearls! I've—I've seen one, once. A long time ago. They're—priceless!"

Bob stared at them, unbelieving. "Tonga pearls," he echoed. "Imagine——"

Everyone had heard of Tonga pearls—but very few had ever seen one. And here were thirteen of them, enormous and perfect! They were the most precious pearls in the sea—and the most mysterious. For the light that seemed to come from them was no illusion. They actually glowed with a life of their own, a silvery, ghost-like beauty that had never been explained by science. Not even the beds they came from had ever been located. I remembered hearing a submariner talking about them once. "They call them Tonga pearls," he had said, "because the legend is that they come from the Tonga Trench, six miles down. Nonsense, Jim! Oysters don't live below five thousand feet—not big ones, anyway. I've been on the rim of the Tonga Trench—as far down as ordinary edenite could take me—and there's nothing there, Jim, nothing but cold water and dead black mud."

But they came from somewhere, obviously enough—for here were thirteen of them in my hand!

"I'm rich!" crowed Roger Fairfane, half dazed with excitement. "Rich! Each one of them—worth thousands, believe me! And I have thirteen of them!"

"Hold on," I said sharply. The dazed look faded from his eyes. He blinked, then made a sudden grab for my hand. I snatched it away from him.

"They're mine!" he roared. "Blast you, Eden, give them to me! I saw them—never mind that cock-and-bull story of Eskow's! If you won't give them up, my father's lawyers will——"

"Hold on," I said again. "They may not even be real."

Bob Eskow took a deep breath. "They're real," he said. "There's no mistaking that glow. Well, Roger—my father doesn't have any lawyers, but I think all three of us found them. And I think all three of us should share."

"Eskow, you stinking little——"

I stopped Roger quickly, before we all got involved with sea-knives. "Wait! You both forget something—we don't own these. Now yet, anyhow. Somebody lost them; somebody will probably want them back. Maybe we have some sort of salvage rights, but right now the thing for us to do is to turn the whole thing over to the Commandant. He can decide what to do next. Then, if we decide——"

"Hush!"

It was Bob, stopping me almost in the middle of a word.

He was staring over my shoulder, down the beach; his eyes were narrowed and wary.

He whispered: "I'm afraid you're right, Jim. Somebody did lose them! And—somebody's coming to take them back!"

6

The Pearly Eyes

Bob stood pointing toward the sea. The Atlantic lay dark under the thickening dusk, the light of the full moon shimmering on it.

For a moment that was all I saw. Then Bob pointed, and I saw a man wading out of the black water.

Roger said sharply: "Who's that? One of the cadets?"

"No." I knew that was impossible.

The same thought had crossed my own mind—a cadet like ourselves, a straggler from the sub-sea marathon. No one else had any business there, of course.

But he was no cadet.

He wore no sub-sea gear—nothing but swim trunks that had an odd, brightly metallic color. He came striding toward us over the wet sand, and the closer he got the stranger he seemed. Something about him was—strange. There was no other word to describe it.

Moonlight is a thief of color; the polarized light steals reds and greens and washes out all the hues but grays. Perhaps it was only that. But his skin seemed much, much too white, pallid, fishbelly white. The way he walked was somehow odd. It was his flipper-shoes, I thought at first—and then as he came closer, I saw that he wore none. Or if there were any, they were much smaller than ours.

And most of all, there was something quite odd about his eyes. They glowed milky white in the moonlight—like cold pearls, with a velvet black dot of pupil in the center.

Quickly I poured the pearls back into the velvet bag and dropped them back into the edenite cylinder. I screwed the cap back on and the edenite film flickered into bluish light.

The stranger stopped a foot away from me. His queer eyes were fixed on the edenite cylinder. I saw that he wore a long sea knife hung from the belt of his trunks.

He said, breathing hard, almost gasping: "Hello. You have—recovered something that I lost, I see." His voice was oddly harsh and flat. There was no accent, exactly, but he clearly had difficulty with his breathing. That was not surprising, in a man just up out of the water—a long swim can put a hitch in anyone's breathing—but together with those eyes, that colorless skin, he seemed like someone I'd have preferred to meet in broad daylight, with more people around.

Roger said challengingly: "They're ours! You'll have to do better than that if you want the p——"

I stopped him before he could say the word. "If you lost something," I cut in, "no doubt you can describe it."

For a moment his face flashed with strange rage in the moonlight. But then he smiled disarmingly, and I noticed that his teeth looked remarkably fine and white.

"Naturally," he agreed. "Why should I not?" He pointed with a hand that seemed oddly shaped. "But I need not describe my missing property very clearly, since you hold it in your hand. It is that edenite tube."

"Don't give to him," Roger said sharply. "Make him identify himself. Make him prove it's his."

The stranger's clawed hand hesitated near the butt of his sea knife, and the sound of his rasping breath came clear in the night. Curious that he should seem to be shorter of breath now than when he first came to us! But he was gasping and panting as though he had just completed a twenty-mile swim. . . .

"I can identify myself," said the stranger. "My name— my name is Joe Trencher."

"Where are you from?"

"It's a long way from here," he said, and paused to get his breath, looking at us. "I come from Kermadec."

Kermadec! That was where Jason Craken had lived— halfway around the world, four miles under the sea, on a flat-topped sea-mount between New Zealand and the Kermadec Deep. "You're a long way from home, Mr. Trencher," I said.

"Too long," He made a breathless little chuckle. "I'm not used to this dry land! It is not like Kermadec."

Strange how he called it "Kermadec" instead of "Kermadec Dome," I thought. But perhaps it was a local question; and, anyway, there were more important things to think about. "Would you mind explaining what you were doing here?"

"Not at all," he wheezed. "I left Kermadec——" again he called it that—"on a business trip, traveling in my own sea car. You can understand that I am not familiar with these waters. Evidently my sonar gear was defective. At any rate—an hour ago I was cruising on autopilot, toward Sargasso City at five hundred fathoms. The next thing I knew, I was swimming for my life." He looked at us soberly. "I suppose I ran aground, somewhere down there." He nodded toward the moonlit sea. "The edenite tube must have floated to the surface. I'll gladly reward the three of you for helping me recover it, of course. Now, if you'll hand it over——"

He was reaching for it. I stepped back.

Roger Fairfane came between us. "That isn't up to you!" he said sharply. "If you own it, we'll get a reward—from the salvage courts. But you'll have to prove your title to it!"

"I can do that, certainly," wheezed the man who called himself Joe Trencher. "But you can see that I have lost everything except the tube itself in the wreck of my sea car. What sort of proof do you want?"

Bob Eskow had been silent and thoughtful, but now he spoke up.

"For one thing," he said, "you might explain something to us, Mr. Trencher. What happened to your thermo-suit, if you had one?"

"Had one? Of course I had one!" But the stranger was off balance, glowering at us. "I had a thermo-suit and an electrolung—how else could I have survived the crash?"

"Then what did you do with it?"

Trencher convulsed with a sudden fit of coughing. I wondered how much of it was an attempt to cover up. "It—it was defective," he wheezed at last. "I couldn't

46

open the face lens after I reached the surface. I—I was suffocating, so I had to cut it loose and abandon it."

Roger said brutally: "That's a lie, Trencher!"

For a moment I thought the stranger was going to spring at us—all three of us.

He tensed and half-crouched, and his hand was on the butt of his sea-knife again. His breath came in whistling gasps, and the milky, pearly eyes were half-slitted, gleaming evilly in the moonlight.

Then he stood straighter and showed those fine white teeth in a cold smile. He shook his head.

"Your manners, young man," he wheezed, "they need improving. I do not like to be called a liar."

Roger gulped and backed away. "All right," he said placatingly. "I only meant—that is, you have to admit your story isn't very convincing. This tube is very valuable, you know."

"I know," agreed the stranger breathlessly.

I cut in: "If you are really who you say you are, isn't there someone who can identify you?"

He shook his head. Again I noticed the strange dead whiteness of his skin in the moonlight. "I am not known here."

"Well, who were you going to see in Sargasso City? Perhaps we could call there."

His queer eyes narrowed. "I cannot discuss my business there. Still, that is a reasonable request. Suppose you check with Kermadec Dome. I can give you some names there—perhaps the name of my attorney, Morgan Wensley. . . ."

"Morgan Wensley!" I nearly shouted the name. "But that's the same name! That's the name of the man who answered Jason Craken's letter!"

"Craken?"

The stranger from the sea jumped back a step, as though the name had been a kind of threat. "Craken?" he repeated again, crouching as though he thought I would lunge at him, his hand on the sea knife. "What do you ——" he whispered hoarsely, and had to stop for breath. "What do you know of Jason Craken?" He was gasping for air and his slitted eyes were blazing milkily.

I explained, "His son, David, was a cadet here. A friend of mine, in fact—before he was lost. Do you know Mr. Craken?"

The stranger called Joe Trencher shivered, as though the water had chilled him—or as though he had been afraid of the name "Craken." He was frightened—and somehow, his fright made him seem more strange and dangerous than ever.

"I've heard the name," he muttered. His strange eyes were fixed hungrily on the edenite cylinder at my side. "I've no more time to waste. I want my property!"

I said: "If it's yours, tell us what is in it."

Trencher's white face looked ugly for an instant, before he smoothed the anger from it. "The tube contains—a—money——" He hesitated, choking and coughing, looking at us searchingly. "Yes, money. And—and legal papers." He had another coughing spasm. "And—pearls."

"Look at him!" cried Roger. "Can't you see he's just guessing?"

It was true that he did seem to be doubtful, I thought. Still, he had been right enough as far as he went.

I asked: "What kind of pearls?"

"Tonga pearls!" Well, that was easy enough to guess, for a man from Kermadec.

"How many of them?"

The pale face was contorted in an expression of rage and fear. The ragged breathing was the only sound we heard for a moment, while Joe Trencher stared at us.

At last he admitted: "I don't know. I'm acting only as an agent, you see. An agent for Morgan Wensley. He asked me to undertake this trip, and he gave me the tube. I can't give you an itemized list of of its contents, because they belong to him."

"Then it isn't yours!" cried Roger triumphantly.

"I'm responsible for it," Trencher gasped. "I must recover it. Here, you!" He reached toward me. "Give me that!"

For a moment I thought we had come to violence—violence had been in the air all those long minutes. But Bob Eskow jumped between us. He said: "Listen, Trencher, we're going to the Commandant. He'll settle this whole thing. If they belong to you, he'll see that you get them. He will make sure that no one is cheated."

Roger Fairfane grumbled: "I'm not so sure. I'd rather keep them until my Dad's lawyer can tell me what to do." Then he glanced at Trencher's long sea knife. "Oh, all right," he agreed uncomfortably. "Let's go to the commandant."

I turned to Mr. Trencher. He was having trouble with his breathing, but he nodded. "An expedient solution," he gasped. "You needn't think I fear the law. I am willing to trust your Commandant to recognize my rights and see that justice is done. . . ."

He stopped suddenly, staring out to the dark sea.

"Look!" he cried.

We all turned to stare. I heard Bob's voice, as hoarse and breathless as Trencher's own. "What in the sea is that?"

It was hard to tell what we saw. A mile out, perhaps, there was something. Something in the water. I couldn't see it clearly, even in the moonlight. But it was enormous.

For a moment I thought I saw a thick neck lifted out of the water, and a head—that same, immense, reptilian head that I had thought I had seen at the rail of the gym ship. . . .

Something struck me just under the ear, and the world fell away from me.

It didn't really hurt, but for a moment I was paralyzed and I could see and feel nothing.

I wasn't knocked out. I knew that I was falling, but I couldn't move a muscle to catch myself. Some judo blow, I suppose, some clever thrust at a nerve center.

Then the world came back into focus. I heard feet pounding on the hard sand, and the splash of water.

"Stop him, Eskow!" Roger was crying shrilly. "He's got the pearls!"

But Bob was bending over me worriedly. The numbness was beginning to leave my body, and I could feel Bob's exploring fingers moving gently over the side of my head.

"No bones broken," he muttered to himself. "But that shark really clipped you one, while you weren't looking.

Hit you with the edge of his hand, I think. You're lucky, Jim; there doesn't seem to be any permanent damage."

In a minute or two I was able to get up, Bob helping me. My neck was stiff and sore as I moved it, but there were no bones grating.

By the edge of the water Roger stood hungrily staring out at the waves. The stranger who called himself Joe Trencher was gone. Bob said: "He hit you, grabbed the edenite tube and dived for the water. Roger ran after him to tackle him—but when he waved that sea knife Roger stopped cold. Then he dived under the water—and that's the last we saw of him."

Roger heard our voices and came running back to us. "Get up!" he cried. "Keep a watch over the water! He can't get far. He hasn't come up for air yet—but he can't stay under much longer, not without sub-sea gear! I want those pearls back!"

He caught my arm. "Go after him, Eden! Bring back those pearls and I'll give you a half interest in them!"

"You'll have to do better than that," I told him. I was beginning to feel better. "I want Bob counted in. An equal three-way split for all of us, in everything that comes out of this deal. Agreed?"

Roger sputtered for a moment, but at last he gave in. "Agreed. But don't let him get away!"

"All right then," I said. "Here's what we're going to do. All of us will put our sub-sea gear back on—electrolungs and face lenses anyway, I don't suppose we need the thermo-suits. We'll go out on the surface and wait for him to stick his nose up for air. Then we'll surround him and bring him in. You're right about him needing air, Roger—he can't get more than a few hundred yards away without coming up for a breath."

We all quickly checked our face lenses and electrolungs and splashed out through the shallows into the calm Bermuda waves.

"Watch out for that sea knife!" I called, and then all three of us were swimming, spreading out, searching the surface of the sea for the pale face and gleaming eyes of the stranger.

Minutes passed.

I could see Roger to my left and Bob Eskow to my right, treading water, staring around. And that was all.

More minutes. I saw nothing. In desperation, I pulled my legs up, bent from the waist and surface-dived to see what was below. It was a strangely frightening experience. I was swimming through ink, swimming about in the space between the worlds where there is neither light nor gravitation. There was no up and no down; there was no sign of light except an occasional feeble flicker of phosphorescence from some marine life. I could easily have got lost and swum straight down. That was a danger; to counter it, I stopped swimming entirely and took a deep breath and held it. In a moment I felt the wash of air across my back and shoulders, as the buoyancy of my lungs lifted me to the surface.

I lifted my head and looked around.

Bob Eskow was shouting and splashing, a hundred yards to my right. And cutting toward him, close to where I had surfaced, Roger Fairfane was swimming with frantic speed.

"Come on!" cried Roger, panting. "Bob's found him, I think!" That was all I had to hear. I drove through the water as fast as my arms and flipper-shoes would take me. But I had breath enough left over to cry out:

"Careful, Bob! Watch out for his knife!"

We got there in moments, and the three of us warily surrounded a feebly floating form in the water.

Knife? There was no knife.

There were no pearly eyes, no milk-white face.

We looked at the figure, and at each other, and without a word the three of us caught hold of him and swam rapidly toward the shore.

We dragged the inert body up on the sand.

I couldn't help staring back at the sea and shivering. What mysteries it held! That strange, huge head—the white-eyed man who had clipped me and stolen the pearls—where were they now?

And what was this newest and strangest mystery of all?

For the inert body that we brought up wasn't Joe Trencher. We all recognized him at once.

It was David Craken, unconscious and apparently more than half drowned.

7

Back from the Deeps

Bob's voice was filled with astonishment and awe. Even Roger Fairfane stood gawking. No wonder! I could hardly believe it myself. When a man is lost on a lung dive at thirteen hundred feet, you don't expect him to be found drifting off shore months later—and still alive!

"Don't stand there!" I cried. "Help me, Bob! We'll give him artificial respiration. Roger, you stand by to take over!"

We dragged him up to the firm, dry sand and flipped him over. Bob knelt beside his head, taking care that his tongue did not choke him, while I spread his arms and moved them, wing fashion, up and down, up and down——

It was hardly necessary. We had barely begun when Davd rolled over suddenly, coughing. He tried to sit up.

"He's alive!" cried Roger Fairfane. "Jim, you keep an eye on him. I'm going after an ambulance and a sea medic. I'll report to the Commandant and——"

"Wait!" cried David Craken weakly. He propped himself on one arm, gasping for breath. "Please. Please don't report anything—not yet."

He gripped my arm with surprising strength and lifted himself up. Roger glanced at him worriedly, then, uneasily, out toward the dark sea, where that peculiar person who had said his name was Trencher had vanished with the pearls. "But we have to report this," he said, without conviction. It was, in fact, an open question—there was nothing in the regulations to cover anything like this.

"Please," said David again. He was shivering from the chill of the deep water, and exhausted as if from a long swim, but he was very much alive. The straps at his shoulders showed where his electrolung had been seated— lost, apparently, after he had surfaced. He said: "Don't report anything. I—I'm lost, according to the Academy's roster. Leave it that way."

Bob demanded: "What happened, David? Where have you been?"

David shook his head, watching Roger. Roger stood irresolutely for a moment, staring at David, then at the lights of the Academy. At last he said: "All right, Craken. Have it your way. But I ought to get a sea medic——"

David choked, but managed a grin. "I don't need a sea medic," he said. "I'm not coming back as a cadet, you see. I'm here on business—for my father. I was in a sea car and I was attacked, down there." He nodded toward the black water. "Subsea pirates," he cried angrily. "They jumped my sea car and robbed me. I was lucky to get away with my life."

"Pirates!" Roger was staring at him. "In the front yard of the Academy! Craken, we've got to do something about this. What did they look like? How many were there? What kind of sea car were they using? Give me the facts, Cracken—I'll get a report to the Fleet, and we'll——"

"Wait, Roger. Wait!" David protested desperately. "I don't want the Fleet. There's nothing they can do to help me now. And I—I can't let anyone know I'm here."

Roger looked at him suspiciously. Then he stared at Bob and me. I could see his brain working, could see the conclusion he was coming to.

"You don't want the Fleet," he said slowly. "You can't let anyone know you're here. Could that be——" he leaned down, staring into David's eyes angrily—"could that be because of what you lost when you were robbed?"

David said weakly, "I—I don't know what you're talking about."

"But you do, Craken! I'd bet a summer's leave you do! Was it pearls you lost when they robbed you, Craken? Thirteen pearls, Tonga pearls, in an edenite tube?"

There was a moment's silence.

Then David got to his feet, his face blank. He said in a cold, changed voice:

"They're mine. Where are they?"

"I thought so!" cried Roger. "What do you think of that, Eden? I knew it was just too much of a coincidence for Craken to turn up right now. He's connected with that Joe Trencher, that stole my pearls!"

David stood up straight. For a moment I thought he was angry, but the expression in his eyes was not rage. He said: "Trencher? Did you say—Trencher?"

"That's the name! As if you didn't know. A queer little white-skinned man, with a case of asthma, I think. Trencher. Don't try to tell us you never heard of him!"

David laughed sharply. "If only I could, Roger," he said soberly. "If only I could! But I must admit that I've heard of him—of them, at any rate. Trencher isn't a name, you see. Trencher is—from the Trench. The Tonga Trench!"

He shook his head. "Joe Trencher. Yes, he would give a name like that. And you met him?"

I cut in. "We not only met him, David, but I'm afraid we let him get away with the pearls." I gave him a quick outline of what had happened, from the moment Bob Eskow felt the edenite cylinder wash against his foot until the stranger clipped me, grabbed it and dived into the sea. "He never came up," I told David Craken. "No electrolung, no thermosuit—but he never came up. I suppose he must be drowned out there now. . . ."

"Drowned? Him?" David Craken looked at me queerly, but then he shook his head again. "No, he isn't drowned, Jim. Trust him for that. I'll explain sometime—but the likes of Joe Trencher will never drown." He looked soberly out to sea. "I thought I'd got away from them," he said. "All this long way from Kermadec Dome. But they caught up with me. I suppose it was inevitable that they would. The first thing I knew was when the microsonar showed something approaching—fast and close. A projectile exploded, I suppose—anyway, the next thing that happened was that my sea car was out of control and taking in water. Those devils came in through the emergency hatches. I got away—but they got the pearls." He sighed. "I needed those pearls," he said. "It isn't just money. I was going to sell them to—to buy something for my father. Something that he has to have."

Roger demanded: "Where did you get the pearls? You've got to tell us that. Otherwise, Craken, I'm warning you—I'm going to report this whole thing!"

"Hold on a minute, Roger!" I interrupted. "There's no sense blackmailing David!"

David Craken smiled at me, then looked at Roger Fairfane. "Blackmail is the word," he said. "But bear this in mind, Roger. *I'll never tell you where the Tonga pearls come from.* Men have died trying to find that out—I won't tell. Is that perfectly clear?"

"Listen," Roger blustered, "you needn't think you can scare me! My father is an important man! You've heard of Trident Lines, haven't you? My father is one of the biggest executives of the line! And if I tell my father——"

"Wait a minute," said David Craken. His tone was oddly placating. He suddenly seemed struck with a thought. "Trident Lines, you say?"

"That's right!" sneered Roger. "I thought that would straighten you out! You can't buck Trident Lines!"

"No, no," David said impatiently. "But—Trident Lines. They're one of the big subsea shippers, aren't they?"

"The third biggest line in the world," said Roger Fairfane with pride.

David Craken took a deep breath. "Roger," he said, "if you're interested in the Tonga pearls, perhaps we can work something out. I—I need help." He turned to us, imploringly. "But not from the Fleet! I don't want anything reported!"

Roger said, puffed with pride now that things seemed to be going his way: "Perhaps that won't be necessary, Craken. What do you want?"

David hesitated. "I—I want to think it over. I came here to do something for my father, and without the pearls, I can't do it—unless I have some help. But first we'd better get out of sight. Is there any place we can go to talk this over?"

Roger said: "There's a beach house about a mile below here—the Atlantic manager of Trident Lines maintains it. He isn't there, but he told me I could use it any time." He said it proudly.

"That will do," said David. "Can you take me there?"

"Well—I suppose so," said Roger, somewhat unwillingly. "Do you think it's necessary? I mean, are you

55

that worried about someone from the Academy seeing you?"

David looked worriedly out to sea, then at Roger.

"It isn't anyone from the Academy that I'm worried about," he told Roger Fairfane.

We made our arrangements. We left David waiting for us in a boathouse on the beach, and Roger, Bob and I hurried back to the Academy to sign in. Every swimmer who completed the marathon was entitled to an overnight pass as a reward, so there was no difficulty getting off the reservation. The cadet on guard, stiffly at attention in his sea-red dress uniform, gave our passes only a glance, but he examined the little bag Roger was carrying very carefully. "Civilian clothes?" he demanded. "What are you going to do with those?"

"They—ah—they need cleaning," Roger said, not untruthfully. "There's a good cleaner in Hamilton."

The guard winked. "Pass, cadets," he said, and returned to stiff attention. Still and all, I didn't feel safe until we were out of sight of the gates. Roger hadn't actually *said* we were gong to Hamilton—but he had certainly said enough to make the guard at the gate start asking questions if he saw us duck off the road in another direction.

We got back to the beach easily enough, and found David waiting. I was almost surprised to see him there—it would have been so easy to believe the whole thing was a dream if he had been gone. But he was there, big as life, and we waited while he got into Roger's dry clothes.

And then the four of us headed down the beach toward the ornate beach house that belonged to the Atlantic manager of Trident Lines.

Overhead there was a ripping, screaming sound—the night passenger jet for the mainland. It was a common enough sound; Bob and Roger and I hardly noticed it. But David stopped still in his tracks, frozen, his face drawn.

He looked at me and grinned, shamefaced. "It's only an airliner, isn't it? But I just can't get used to them. We don't have them in Marinia, you see."

Roger muttered something—I suppose it was a contemptuous reference to David Craken's momentary nervousness—and stalked down the beach ahead of us. He seemed nervous himself about something, I thought. I said: "David, don't mind him. We're glad to see you back. Even Roger. It's just his—his——"

"His desire to get hands on the Tonga pearls?" David finished for me, and grinned. He seemed more relaxed, though I couldn't help noticing that his eyes never went far from the cold black sea. "I can't blame him for that. They're fabulously valuable, of course. Even somebody whose father is a high executive of Trident Lines might want to get a couple of Tonga pearls to put away against a rainy day."

I said, trying to be fair: "I don't think it's only that, David. Roger always wants to—to win, I guess. It's important to him. Remember the diving tests, when he carried on so? Remember——"

I stopped, staring at him.

"That reminds me," I said. "Don't you have some explaining to do about that?"

He said seriously, "Jim, believe me, I'll answer every question I can—even that one. But not now." He hesitated, and lowered his voice. "I was kidnaped from the gym ship, Jim. Kidnaped by the same person who called himself 'Joe Trencher.' "

I stared at him. "Kidnaped? At a depth of thirteen hundred feet? But that's impossible, David! How could any human being do it—why, it would take a sea car and heaven knows what else to do a thing like that!"

David Craken looked at me, his eyes bright and serious in the moonlight.

"Jim," he said, "what makes you think that Joe Trencher is human?"

8

The Half Men

Roger called it a "beach house"—but it was two stories tall, a sprawling mansion with ten acres of sub-tropical gardens and a dozen outbuildings.

The whole estate was surrounded by a twenty-foot hedge of prickly thorns and tiny red flowers. A land crab might have been able to squirm through the hedge, but no human being could. Roger led us to a gate in the hedge, ten feet high, with carved metal doors, the hedge growing together solidly above it. The doors were wide open, and no one was in sight.

But it was not unguarded.

"Halt!" rattled a peremptory mechanical voice. "Halt! You, there! Where are you going and what do you want?" The doors moved uneasily, though there was no wind. It was as though they were anxious to crash shut on the intruders.

"It's the automatic watchman," Roger explained, a little nervously. He cried: "I am Roger Fairfane. I have permission to come in."

The mechanical voice crackled: "Roger Fairfane. Step forward!" There was a momentary hiss and a rustle of static, as though the invisible electronic brain were scanning its library of facts to find out if the name Roger Fairfane was on the list of permitted visitors.

Roger took a step forward and a beam of sizzling red light leaped down at him from a projector on the side of the gate. In its light he looked changed and ghastly, and a little scared.

The mechanical voice rattled: "Roger Fairfane, you have permission to go to the boathouse. Follow the indicated path." It clicked, and the faint hum from the loudspeaker died. The doors shuddered one more time, as if regretful that they could not close, and then were still.

A line of violet Troyon lights, rice-grain sized, lit up

along the ground, outlining a path that led through palms and clumps of hibiscus toward the water.

"Come along, come along," said Roger hurriedly. "Stay on the path!"

We followed the curving coral walk outlined by the flecks of violet light. The boathouse turned out to be as big as an average-sized dwelling. There was a basin for a private sub-sea cruiser, and with a house built around it, an apartment on the upper floor. Another beam of reddish light leaped out at us from over the entrance as we approached. It singled out Roger Fairfane, and in a moment the door opened.

We walked in, the door closing behind us. It was uncomfortably like a trap.

The first thing to do was get something to eat—not only for David, but for all of us; we hadn't eaten since the marathon swim. Roger disappeared into the kitchen of the little apartment and we could hear him struggling with the controls of the electronic housekeeper. He came out after a moment with a tray of milk and sandwiches. "The best I can do," he said, a little grumpily. "This apartment belongs to the pilot of the sea-car, and it isn't too well stocked."

It was good enough for all of us, though. We demolished the sandwiches and then sat before a roaring fire in the fireplace, which had kindled itself as we came into the room. If this was the pilot's apartment, what would the master's home be like! We all were impressed with the comfort and luxury that surrounded us—even Roger.

Then we talked.

David put down the last of his sandwich and sat staring at us for a moment.

"It's hard to know where to begin," he said at last.

"Start with the Tonga pearls," Roger suggested shortly.

David looked at him, and then at Bob and me, with his eyes dark with trouble.

"Before I tell you anything," he said at last, "you must promise me something. Promise you won't repeat what I'm going to tell you to anyone, without my permission. Especially, promise you won't report anything to the Fleet."

Roger said promptly: "Agreed!"

David looked at me. I hesitated. "I'm not sure we should promise," I told him slowly. "After all, we're cadets, in training for Fleet commissions. . . ."

"But we haven't got them yet!" objected Roger. "We haven't taken the oath."

Bob Eskow was frowning over some private thought. He seemed about to say something, then changed his mind.

David Craken looked hard at me. His voice was very clear and firm. "Jim, if you can't promise to keep your mouth shut, I'll have to ask you to leave. There's too much depending on me. I need help badly—but I can't afford to take a chance on word getting out." He hesitated. "It—it's a matter of life and death, Jim. My father's life."

Roger snapped. "Listen, Jim, there's no problem here. David isn't asking you to violate an oath—you haven't even taken it! Why can't you just go along and promise?"

David Craken held up his hand. "Wait a minute, Roger." He turned to me again. "Suppose I ask you," he said, "to promise to keep this conversation secret *as long as it does not conflict with your duty to the Fleet*. And to promise if you report anything I say, that you'll talk it over with me beforehand."

I thought it over, and that seemed reasonable enough. But before I could speak Bob Eskow stood up. His expression had cleared magically. "Speaking for myself," he said, "that's fine. Let's shake on it all around!"

Solemnly we all clasped hands.

Roger demanded: "Now, where did you get the pearls?"

David grinned suddenly. He said: "Don't be impatient. Do you know, Roger, I could tell you exactly where they came from. I could pinpoint the location of a subsea chart and give you an exact route to get there. And believe me, it would be useless to you. Worse than useless." The grin vanished. "You see, Roger," he went on, "you would never come back alive."

He leaned back and looked into the flames. "My father is an expert benthologist. A scientist of the deeps. He made his reputation many years ago, before I was born, and under another name. As a benthologist, he went on many sub-sea exploring missions—and on one of them discovered the oyster beds that produce the Tonga pearls." He paused, and, in a different tone, added: "I wish he never had. The pearls are—dangerous."

Roger said aggressively: "You're talking about those silly legends? Rot! Just superstition. There have been stories about gems being unlucky for thousands of years—but the only bad luck is not having them!"

David Craken shook his head. "The Tonga pearls have caused a lot of trouble," he said. "Perhaps some of it was merely because they were so valuable and so—so lovely. But believe me, there is more to it than that. They caused the death of every man on that expedition except one, my father."

Bob cut in: "Do you mean they killed each other for the pearls?"

"Oh, no! They were all good men—scientists, explorers, sub-sea experts. But the pearl beds are well guarded. That's why no one else has ever got back from the Tonga beds to report their location."

"Wait a minute," I interrupted. "Guarded? Guarded by what?"

David looked at me, frowning doubtfully.

"Jim, you've got to remember that most of the ocean is still as strange as another planet. There's three times as much of the ocean bottom as all the dry land on Earth put together. And it's harder to explore. We can travel about, we can search with fathometers and microsonar—but what is the extreme range of our search? It's like trying to map Bermuda from an airplane, during a thunderstorm. We can see patches, we can penetrate through the clouds with radar—but only big, broad outlines come through. There are things under the sea that—that you wouldn't believe."

I wanted to interrupt again, to ask him if he meant that terrible saurian head I had seen at the railing of the gym ship—or the mystery of his own disappearance and return —or the strange eyes of the being who called himself Joe Trencher. But something held me silent as he went on.

"The ship was lost," David said. "My father got away in his diving gear, with the first batch of pearls. I think— I think he should properly have reported what happened to the expedition. But he didn't." He frowned, as though trying to apologize for his father. "You see, times were different then. The conquest of the sub-sea world was just beginning. There was no Sub-sea Fleet; piracy was common. He knew that he would lose his right of discovery—might even have lost his life—if the secret of the pearls got out.

"So—he didn't report.

"He changed his name, to Jason Craken. The Kraken—spelled with a K—is the old name for the fabulous monsters of the deep. It was very appropriate, as you will see. He took the pearls he had managed to save, and sold them, a few at a time, very carefully, in ways that were not entirely legal. But he had no choice, you see."

David sat up straighter, his eyes beginning to flash, his voice growing stronger. "Then—well, I told you he was an expert benthologist. He invented a new technique—a way of harvesting more pearls, without being killed. Believe me, it wasn't easy. All these years he has been harvesting the Tonga pearl beds——"

"All alone!" cried Roger Fairfane. He pushed back his chair and leaped up, striding back and forth. "One man harvesting all the Tonga pearls! What an opportunity!"

David looked at him. "An opportunity—more than that, Roger," he said. "For he was not quite alone. He had—well, call them employees—to protect him and help him harvest the pearls."

Bob Eskow was standing up. "Wait a minute! I thought you said your uncle was the only man who knew the secret of the Tonga beds."

David nodded. For a moment he was silent. Then he said:

"The employees were not men."

"Not men! But——"

"Please, Bob. Let me tell this my way." Bob shrugged and sat down; David went on. "My father built himself a home near the pearl beds—a sub-sea fort, really armored with edenite. He gathered a lot of pearls. They were fabulously valuable, and they were all his. He built a new identity for himself in the sub-sea cities so that he could sell the pearls. He made a lot of money."

David's eyes looked reminiscent and faintly sad.

"While my mother was alive, we lived luxuriously. It was a wonderful, fantastic life, half in the undersea cities, half in our own secret dome. But—my mother died. And now everything has changed."

His voice had a husky catch, and his thin face turned very white. I noticed that his hands were trembling just a little, but he went on.

"Everything has changed. My father is an old man now—and sick, besides. He can't rule his—his employees the way he used to. His undersea empire is slipping out of his hands. The people he used to trust have turned against him. He has no one else. That's why we must have help!"

Excitement was shining in Bob's eyes and Roger's, and I could feel my own pulse racing. A secret fortress guarding a hidden undersea empire! Tonga pearls, glowing like moons in the dark! The challenge of unknown dangers under the sea! It was like a wonderful adventure story, and it was happening to us, here in this little apartment over the empty boathouse!

I said: "David, what kind of help do you need?"

He met my eyes squarely. "Fighting help, Jim! There is danger—my father's life isn't worth a scrap of Tonga oystershell unless I can bring him help. We need——" he hesitated before saying it—"we need a fighting ship, Jim. An armed subsea cruiser!"

That stopped us all.

We stared at him as though he were a lunatic. I said: "A *cruiser*? But—but, David, private citizens can't use a Fleet cruiser! Why not just call on the Fleet? If it's that serious——"

"No! My father doesn't want the Fleet!"

We looked at him helplessly.

David grinned tightly. "I'm not crazy. He doesn't want to give away the location of the pearl beds. He would lose everything he has. And besides—there are the—the creatures in that part of the sea. They would have to be killed if the Fleet comes in. And my father doesn't want to kill them."

"Creatures? What creatures?" I asked it, but I think I knew the answer before hand. For I could not forget the enormous scaled head I had seen over the rail of the gym ship.

David waved the question aside. "I'll explain," he said, "when I know if you can help me. For I haven't much time. My father's—call them employees—have turned against him. They've cut him off and surrounded him, down in his sub-sea fort. We must have a fighting ship and fighting men to rescue him. And there isn't much time."

He stood up, staring at us intently. "But not the Fleet!"

"What then?" asked Roger Fairfane, puzzled.

David said, "Have you ever heard of the subsea cruiser *Killer Whale?*"

We looked at each other. The name sounded a tiny echo for all of us—somewhere we had heard it, somewhere recently.

I got it first. "Of course," I cried. "The Fleet surplus sale! Down in Sargasso City—there are two of them, aren't there? Two obsolete subsea cruisers, and they're going to be sold for salvage. . . ."

David nodded, then checked himself and shook his head. "Almost right, Jim," he said. "But there is really only one ship. The other one—the *Dolphin*—it's only a heap of rust. The *Killer Whale* is the ship I want. True, I would have to find armament for it somewhere. The Fleet would sell it stripped. But it's a serviceable vessel. My father knows it well; it was based in Kermadec Dome a few years ago. If I could arm it—and man it with three or four good men——"

Bob said excitedly: "We could help you, David! We've completed enough courses in subsea tactics and battle maneuvers—we've all of us had training in simulated combat! But the price, David! Those things, even scrapped, would cost a fortune!"

David nodded. He said somberly, "We figured it out, my father and I. They would cost just about as much as a handful of Tonga pearls."

We were all silent for a moment. Then Roger Fairfane raised his head and laughed sharply.

"So you've been wasting our time," he said. "You've lost the pearls. There's no way of getting the money without them."

David looked at him thoughtfully. "No way?" He

paused, trying to find the right words. "You said you would help, Roger. And your father—a wealthy man, an important man in Trident Lines. . . ."

Roger flushed angrily. "Leave my father out of this!" he ordered.

David nodded, unsurprised. "I rather thought it would be like that," he said calmly. He didn't explain that remark, but Roger seemed to understand. He turned bright red, then pale with anger, but he kept quiet. David said:

"I knew there was some danger. Joe Trencher was once my father's foreman, and now that he is leading the revolt against my father, we knew what to expect. My father told me there was a good chance that Trencher would find some way of getting the pearls away from me."

"And did he tell you what to do in that case?" Roger sneered.

David nodded. He looked at me. "He said, 'Ask for help. Go to see Jim Eden, and ask his uncle for help.'"

I couldn't have been more surprised if he had turned into one of these strange sub-sea saurians before my eyes.

"My uncle Stewart? But—but——"

David said: "That's all I know, Jim. My father's sick, as I said. And perhaps he was a little delirious. But that is what he said."

I shook my head, thinking hard. "But—but——" I said again. "But—my uncle is in Marinia. More than ten thousand miles from here. And he isn't too well himself.'

David shrugged, looking suddenly tired. "That's all I know, Jim," he repeated. "The only thing——"

He broke off, listening. "What's that?"

We all stopped and listened. Yes, there had been something—some faint mechanical whisper. It sounded like powerful muffled motors, not too far away.

Bob jumped up. "The sea-car basin! It's coming from there!"

It was hard to believe—but it *did* sound that way. All four of us leaped up and raced out of the little apartment, down the steps, onto the platform that surrounded the little basin where the Atlantic manager's subsea vessel was moored when he was present.

There was nothing there. We looked around in the glow of the violet Troyon lights. There was the little railed landing, the white walls, the face of the water itself. Nothing else, But—the sea doors stood wide open.

We stared out through the open doors, to where the waters inside the basin joined the straight, narrow canal that led to the open sea. There were waves, shrunken imitations of the breakers outside; there were ripples bouncing off the sides.

There was no sign of a sea car.

David Craken said wearily: "I wonder—— No, it couldn't be."

"What couldn't be?" I asked.

He shrugged. "I guess I'm hearing ghosts. For a moment I thought, just possibly, Joe Trencher had followed us here—come into the basin, listened to what we were saying. But it can't be true." He pointed to the silent scanning ports of the electronic watchman. "Anything that came in or out would trip the search circuits," he reminded us. "The electronic watchman didn't sound an alarm—so it couldn't have been that."

Bob Eskow said stubbornly: "I'm *sure* I heard motors."

David said: "I was sure too—but don't you see it's impossible? I suppose we heard some strange echo from the surf—or perhaps a surface boat passing, well out to sea——"

Bob Eskow glowered. "I'm no lubber, David! I know the sound of sea-car motors when I hear them!" But then he hesitated and looked confused. "But you're right," he admitted. "It couldn't have been that. The electronic watchman would have spotted it at once."

We trudged back upstairs, but somehow the mood of excitement that had possessed us was gone. We were all looking a little thoughtful, almost worried.

It was getting late, anyhow. We quickly made plans for what we had to do. "I'll try to call my uncle," I said. "—I don't know what good it will do. But I'll try. Meanwhile, David, I suppose you might as well stay here and keep out of sight. We've got to get back to the Academy, but tomorrow we'll come back and then——"

"Then we'll get to work," Bob promised.

And that was all for that strange, exciting day . . . except for one thing.

We left David there and walked slowly back through the fairy garden to the gate. We were all feeling tired by then—bone-tired, exhausted, not only from the strenuous activity of the marathon swim but from the letdown after our strange meeting with David Craken and with Joe Trencher, whoever he was.

Maybe that was why we were out of the garden and a hundred yards down the road before I noticed something.

I stopped still in the coral road. "You closed the gate!" I said sharply to Bob.

He looked around. "Why—yes, I did. I pushed it closed as we came through. After all, I didn't want to leave it open in case some——"

"No, no!" I cried. "You *closed* it! Remember? It was standing half ajar. Don't you see what I mean? Come on—follow me!"

Tired as I was, I trotted back to the gate. It was closed, all right, just as Bob had left it. There was the twenty-foot high hedge, thorny and impenetrable. There was the gate, with the monitoring turret of the electronic watchman at the side.

We stopped in front of the gate, panting.

Nothing happened.

"You see?" I cried. They blinked at me.

"Don't you understand *yet?* Watch me " I pushed the gate open. It swung wide.

Nothing else happened.

Roger Fairfane got it then—and a moment later, Bob Eskow caught on.

"The electronic watchman!" Bob whispered. "It—it isn't on! That's an automatic gate—you shouldn't be able to move it, unless the red scanning ray identifies you. . . ."

I nodded.

"Now you see," I told them. "The watchmen's been turned off—somehow. It isn't working. Wires cut, I suppose."

Roger looked at me worriedly.

"So—so those motors we thought we heard down below——"

I nodded. "It wasn't imagination," I said. "They were real. They disconnected the watchman and came in. And every word we said, they overheard."

9

Sargasso Dome

Eastward and down. Our destination was Sargasso City.

Neither Bob nor Roger Fairfane could get a pass; it was up to David and me to go to Sargasso City and look over the *Killer Whale.* We argued for a long time whether it was safe for David to come along—if a cadet should see him and recognize him, there would be questions asked! But it seemed that there should be two of us, and that left us no choice.

We booked passage from Hamilton on the regular subsea shuttle to Sargasso City, a hundred and fifty miles east of Bermuda and more than two miles straight down. In the short time before our subsea ship left I found a phone booth and placed a long-distance call to my uncle Stewart in far-off Thetis Dome.

There was no answer.

I told the operator: "Please, it's very important. Can you keep trying?"

"Certainly, sir!" She was all professional competence. "Give me your number, please. I'll call you back."

I thought rapidly. That was impossible, of course—I wouldn't be there for more than a few more minutes. Yet I didn't want to have my uncle phone me at the Academy, since there was the chance that someone might overhear. I said: "Keep trying, operator. I'll call you from Sargasso Dome in——" I glanced at my watch—"in about two hours."

David was gesticulating frantically from outside the booth. I hung up and the two of us raced down the long gloomy shed that was the Pan-Carib Line's dock. We just reached the ship as the gangways were about to come down.

I couldn't help feeling a little worried for no good reason—naturally, my uncle had plenty to do with his time! There was nothing much to worry about if he wasn't at home at any particular moment. Still, it was halfway around the world and rather late at night in Thetis Dome; I felt a nagging doubt in the back of my mind that everything was well with him. . . .

But the joy of cruising the deeps again put it out of my mind in a matter of moments.

We slid away from Hamilton port on the surface. As soon as we were safely past the shallows of the shelf we dived cleanly beneath the waves and leveled on course for Sargasso Dome.

The little shuttle vessel was a midget beside the giant Pacific liners in which I had traveled to Thetis Dome long before, but it was two hundred feet long for all of that. Because it was small, discipline was free and easy, and David and I were able to roam the crew spaces and the enginerooms without much trouble. It made the time pass quickly. At seventy knots the entire voyage took a little less than two hours; the time was gone before we knew it.

We disembarked at Sargasso City through edenite coupler tubes and immediately looked for a phone booth.

I poured coins into it, and got the same operator once more by dialing her code number.

There was still no answer.

I left the call in, and David and I asked directions to the Fleet basin where the surplus ships lay idle, waiting to be sold at public auction.

The *Killer Whale* lay side by side with the old *Dolphin* in the graving docks at the bottom of Sargasso Dome.

Neither was particularly big—they'd both been small enough to fit in the ship lock that let them into the city from the cold deeps outside. But the *Dolphin* seemed like a skiff next to the *Killer Whale*. We didn't waste time looking at her; we quickly boarded the *Killer* through the main hatch and examined her from stem to stern.

David looked up at me, his eyes glistening. "She's a beauty," he whispered.

I nodded. The *Killer Whale* was one of the last Class-K subsea cruisers built. There was nothing wrong with her, nothing at all, except that in the past ten years there had been so many improvements in subsea weapons—requiring different mounts, different design from stem to stern—that the Fleet had condemned every vessel more than a decade old. The process of conversion was nearly complete, and only a few old-timers like the *Dolphin* and the *Killer Whale* still remained to be replaced.

There were crew quarters for sixteen men. "We'll rattle around in her," I told David. "But we can handle her. One of us on the engines and one at the controls; we can split up and take twelve-hour shifts. She'll run like a dream, you'll see."

He put his hand on the master's wheel as though he were touching a holy object. "She's a beauty," he said again. "Well, let's go up and see about putting in a bid."

That took a little bit of the spell off the moment for both of us. Putting in a bid—but what did we have to bid with? Unless my uncle Stewart could help—and he was very far from being a rich man—we couldn't raise the price of the little escape capsule the *Whale* carried in her bilges, much less the cost of the whole cruiser.

In the office of the lieutenant-commander in charge of disposing of the two vessels we were informed that the rock-bottom bid that would be accepted was fifty thousand dollars. The officer looked us over and grinned. "Pretty expensive to buy out of your allowances, boys," he said. "Why don't you settle for something a little smaller—say, a toy sailboat?"

For the first time in my life I regretted wearing the dress scarlet uniform of an Academy cadet—in civilian clothes, I would have felt a lot freer to tell him what I thought! David stepped in front of me to avert the explosion.

"How do we go about putting in a bid?" he asked.

The officer lost a little of his amused look. "Why," the said, "if you're serious about this, all you have to do is take one of these application forms and fill it in. Put down your name and address and the amount you're prepared to bid. You'll have to post a bond of one-third of the amount you're bidding before the bids are opened, otherwise your bid won't even be considered. That's all there is to it."

"May I have a form for the *Killer Whale* then, sir?"

The lieutenant commander looked at him, then shrugged. "*Killer,* eh?" he said, scrabbling through the pile of forms on his desk. "You're smart there, anyway. The *Dolphin's* nothing but a heap of rust. I ought to know—I served in her myself, as an ensign. But what in the world do you want a cruiser for, young man—even if you had the money to pay for it?"

David coughed. "I—I want it for my father," he said, and quickly took the forms from the officer's hand.

We retired to the outer office, clutching the forms.

It was a big, public room, full of people, some of whom looked at us curiously. We found a corner where we could go over the papers.

I looked over David's shoulder. The forms were headed *Application for Purchase of Surplus Subsea Vessel,* and on the first page was a space where the names of the *Killer Whale* and the *Dolphin* had been filled in for us. David promptly put a big check mark next to the *Killer Whale.* He filled in my name and address and hesitated over the space marked: *Amount offered.*

I stopped him.

"Hold on a second," I said. "Let me try calling my uncle again. There's phone booth right across the room."

He grinned. "Might as well see if we're going to be able to pay for it," he agreed.

This time my call went right through.

But the person who answered was not my uncle.

It was a vision-phone, and the picture before my eyes swirled and cleared and took form. It was Gideon Park—my uncle's most trusted helper, the man who had saved my life in the drains under Thetis Dome so long ago!

His black face looked surprised, then grinned, his teeth flashing white. "Young Jim! It's good to see you, boy!" Then he looked oddly concerned. "I guess you want your uncle, eh? He's—uh—he can't be reached right now, Jim. Can I help you? You're not in trouble at the Academy, are you?"

"No, nothing like that, Gideon. Where is my uncle?"

He hesitated. "Well, Jim——"

"Gideon! What's the matter? Is anything wrong?"

71

He said, "Now, hold on, Jim. He's going to be all right. But he's—well, he's sleeping right now. I've had the phone disconnected all day so as not to disturb him, and I don't want to wake him up unless——"

"Gideon, tell me what's wrong with my uncle!"

He said soberly: "It isn't too bad, I promise you that, Jim. But the truth is, he's sick."

"Sick!"

Gideon nodded, the black face worried and sympathetic. "He had some sort of an attack. Three days ago it was. He got a letter from an old acquaintance of his. He was reading it, right here at his desk, when suddenly he keeled over——"

"A heart attack?"

Gideon shook his head. He said in his soft, warm voice: "Nothing so simple, Jim. All the sea-medics say is that your uncle has been under too much pressure. He has lived too deep, too long."

That was true enough, no doubt of it. I remembered my uncle's long, exciting life in the Deeps. The time when he had been trapped—just a few months back—in a crippled ship at the bottom of the deepest trench in the southwest Pacific. His recovery had seemed complete, when Gideon and I found him and brought him back— but the human body was not evolved for the life of a deep-sea fish. High pressure and drugs can sometimes have unexpected effects.

"Can I speak to him?"

"Well—the sea-medics say he shouldn't have too much excitement, Jim. Is it—is it anything I can help with?"

I only paused a second—I knew I could trust Gideon as much as my uncle himself. I began to pour out the whole mixed-up story of the pearly-eyed men and the Tonga pearls and David Craken——

"Craken? Did you say David Craken?"

I stopped, staring at Gideon through the viewscreen. "Why, yes, Gideon. His father's name is Jason Craken—" or that's what he calls himself."

"A queer thing! Craken, Jim—that's the letter that came! The letter your uncle was reading when he had the attack—from Jason Craken!" He hesitated a second.

Then: "Hold on, Jim," he ordered. "Sink the sea-medics—I'll wake him up!"

There was a moment's pause, then a quick shadowy flicker as Gideon transferred the call at his end to an extension in my uncle's bedroom.

I saw my uncle Stewart sitting, propped up, in a narrow bed. His face looked hollow and thin, but he smiled to see me. Evidently he had been lying there awake, for there was no trace of sleepiness in his manner.

"Jim!" His voice seemed hoarse and weary, but strong. "What's this stuff Gideon is telling me?"

Quickly I told him what I had told Gideon—and more, from the moment I had met David Craken on the gym ship until the actual filling out of the bid for purchase of the *Killer Whale*. "And he said to call you, Uncle Stewart," I finished. "And—and so I did."

"I'm glad you did, Jim!" My uncle closed his eyes for a second, thinking, "We've got to help him, Jim," he said at last. "It's a debt of honor."

"A debt?" I stared at the viewscreen. "But I didn't know you ever heard of Jason Craken——"

He nodded. "It's something I never told you, Jim. Years ago, when your father and I were young. We were exploring the rim of the Tonga Trench—as far down as we could go in the diving gear we had then. We were looking for pearls. Tonga pearls."

He nodded. "Tonga pearls," he said again." Well, we found them. But we couldn't keep them, Jim, because while your father and I were out in pressure suits—right at the bottom of the safe limit—we were attacked. I—I can't tell you what attacked us, Jim, because I gave my word. Perhaps the Crakens themselves will tell you sometime. But we were hauled farther and farther down into the deep—far past the rated limits of our armor. It began to fail."

He paused, remembering that far-off day. Oddly, he smiled. "I thought we were done then, Jim," he said. "But we were rescued. The man who rescued us was—Jason Craken.

"Jason Craken!" My uncle was sitting up now, and for a moment his voice was strong. "A strange name—for a strange man! He was short-spoken, almost rude, a little odd. He wore a beard. He dressed like a dandy. He had a taste for luxuries, a lavish spender, a generous host. And a very shrewd man, Jim. He sold Tonga pearls—no one else could compete with him, because no one else knew where they came from. It was worth a fortune to him to keep that monopoly secret, Jim.

"And your father and I—we knew the secret. And he saved our lives.

"He risked his own life to save us—and he endangered the secret of the pearls. But he trusted us. We promised never to come back to the Tonga Trench. We gave our word never to say where the pearls came from.

"And if he needs help now, Jim—it's up to you and me to see that he gets it."

He frowned. "I—I can't do much myself, Jim—I'm laid up for a while. I suppose it was the shock of Jason Craken's letter. But he mentioned that he might need money for a fighting ship, and I've been able to raise some. Not a fortune. But—enough, I think. I'll see that you get it as fast as I can get it to you. Buy the *Killer Whale* for him. Help him any way you can."

He slumped back against the bed and grinned at me. "That's all, Jim. Better sign off now—this call must be costing a fortune! But remember—we owe a lot to Jason Craken, because if it hadn't been for him neither you nor I would be here now."

And that was all.

I turned, a little shaken, to where David was waiting outside the booth.

"It's all right, David," I told him, glancing around the room. "He's going to help. We'll get some money from him—enough, he says. And——"

I broke off. "David!" I cried. "Look—over there, where we were filling out the application forms!"

He whirled. He had left the forms on a little desk to come over while I called my uncle. They were still there—and over them was bending the figure of a man.

Or was it man? For the figure turned and saw us looking at him—saw us with pearly eyes, that contracted and glared. It was the person from the sea who called himself "Joe Trencher"!

74

He turned and ran—through the door, out into the crowded passages beyond. "Come on!" cried David. "Let's catch him—maybe he's still got the pearls!"

10

Tencha of Tonga Trench

We scoured Sargasso City that day—but we never found Joe Trencher.

At the end, David stopped, panting.

"We've lost him," he said. "Once he got out of sight, he was gone."

"But he's got to be in the city somewhere! We can search level by level——"

"No." David shook his head. "He doesn't have to be in the city, Jim. He—isn't like you and me, Jim. He might calmly walk into an escape lock and disappear into the sea, and we'd be spending our next month searching in here while he was a hundred miles away."

"Into the sea? Nearly three miles down? It isn't humanly possible!"

David only said: "Sign the bid form, Jim. We have to get it in."

That was all he would say.

We returned to the lieutenant commander's office. I signed my name to the application form with hardly a glance at it; we put down the minimum bid—fifty thousand dollars. Fifty thousand dollars! But of course the ship had cost many times that, new.

We barely made it back to the subsea shuttle for the return trip to Bermuda.

We were both quiet, and I suppose thinking the same thoughts. Curious, that Joe Trencher should have been able to find us in Sargasso Dome! It made it almost certain that the sound of motors we had heard in the boat basin was indeed Trencher, or someone close to him, listening in on our discussion. So they knew everything we had planned. . . .

But there was no help for it; we couldn't change our plans. There simply was nothing else for us to do.

We sat in silence, in the main passenger lounge, for half an hour or so. We were nearly alone. There was a faint whisper of music from the loud speakers, and a few couples on holiday at the far end of the lounge; and that was all. Business was not brisk between Bermuda and Sargasso City at that particular season.

Finally I could stand it no longer.

I burst out: "David! This has gone far enough. Don't you see, I have to know what we're up against! Who is this Joe Trencher? What's his connection with your father and the Tonga pearls?"

David looked at me with troubled eyes.

Then he glanced around the lounge. No one was near by, no one could hear.

He said at last: "All right, Jim. I suppose it's the best way. I did promise my father—— But he's a sick man, and a long way off. I think I'll have to use my own judgment now."

"You'll tell me about Trencher and—and those sea serpents, or whatever they were?"

He nodded.

"Trencher," he said. "Joe Trencher. He was once my father's foreman. His most trusted employee—and now he is leading the mutineers."

"Mutineers against what, David?" I was more than a little exasperated. So many things I didn't understand—so much mystery that I could not penetrate!

"Mutineers against my father, of course. I told you about my father's dome—about the undersea empire he built out of the Tonga pearls. Well, it's slipping out of his hands now. The helpers he used to trust have turned against him. Trencher is only one."

I couldn't help wondering once more about that "empire" beneath the sea. It didn't seem that David's father could have built it by strictly legal and honest methods—but that was a long time ago, of course. . . .

"It began with the sea serpents," David was saying. "They have lived in the Tonga Trench, made their lairs in the very sea mount where my father built his dome, for millions of years, Jim. Maybe hundreds of millions. You see reconstructions of beasts like them in the museums, and they go back to a time long, long before there were any humans on earth. They're unbelievably ancient, and they haven't changed a bit in all those hundreds of millions of years. Until my father came along. And he—he is trying to do something with them, Jim. Something that's hard to believe. He's trying to train them as horses and dogs are trained—to help him, to work for him. He's trying to domesticate saurians that date back to the age of dinosaurs!"

I stared at him, hardly believing. I remembered that giant, dimly seen head that loomed over the rail of the gym ship. Domesticate *that?* It would be as easy to teach a rattlesnake to carry a newspaper!

But he was still talking.

"Naturally, Dad couldn't do it alone," he said. "But he had help—a curious kind of help, almost as unbelievable as the sea serpents themselves.

"Joe Trencher. And a few hundred others like him. Not very many—but enough. Without them my father couldn't have got to first base with the saurians. Trencher's people were a great help."

"They're ugly enough looking, if Trencher is any sample," I told him. "Those white, pearly eyes—that pale skin. The funny way they breathe. They don't even seem human!"

David nodded calmly. "They aren't," he said. "Not any more, at any rate. They're descended from humans—Polynesians, somehow trapped in a subsidence of land. You've heard of the sea-mounts of the Pacific?"

We nodded, all of us. Those flat-topped submarine mountains, planed level by wave action—yet far below the surface, below any waves.

"Once they were islands," David went on. "And Trencher's ancestors lived on one of them. I suppose they were divers—so far back, it is impossible to tell. But they had Polynesian names, so it couldn't have been too far back. Trencher's own father's name was Tencha—and Trencher took the new name on a whim of Dad's. Trencher. A being from the Tonga Trench.

"And when their island submerged, they somehow

managed to live. They reverted to the past, the far-distant past when every living thing lived in the water."

"You mean——" I hesitated, fumbling for words, hardly able to believe I was hearing right. "You mean Joe Trencher is some sort of—of merman?"

"Dad calls them 'amphibians.' They are mutations. Their lungs are changed to work like gills. They're more at home in the water now, actually, than they are on dry land."

I nodded, remembered all too clearly the panting, wheezing difficulty Joe Trencher had had with breathing air. I began to understand it now.

"Trencher used to be my friend," said David somberly. "When I was at home, I used to put on a lung and dive with him—not down in the Trench, but at a thousand feet or so. I watched him training the—the creatures. He showed me things on the floor of the sea that the Fleet has never seen.

"But then he changed. Dad blames himself. He says the mutation made the amphibians somehow temperamentally unstable, and then, as they learned something about the outside world—they—changed. But whatever it was, now he hates Dad—and all humans. He's the one who kidnaped me from the gym ship. He'd been waiting for his chance—do you remember how many strange little things had been happening, pieces of equipment mysteriously missing, that sort of thing? That was Joe Trencher.

"He turned up, down there at thirteen hundred feet. I—I didn't suspect anything, Jim. I was glad to see him. But I didn't know what had been happening back in my father's dome. I don't know what Trencher did to me—clubbed me, I suppose. I woke up in his sea car, on the way back to Tonga Trench.

"He threatened to kill me, you see. I was his hostage. He used me to threaten my father. But my father's a stubborn man. He has ruled his subsea empire a long time, and he didn't give in."

"Then how did you get away?"

For the first time, David Craken smiled.

"Maeva," he said. "Maeva—my friend. She's just an amphibian girl, but she was loyal. I'd known her since we were both very small. We grew up together. We both watched Joe Trenchor breaking the saurians. Then Maeva and I would go exploring, after—me in my edenite suit, she breathing the water itself. We'd go through the caves in the seamount. I suppose it was dangerous, in a way—those caves belonged to the saurians; they laid their eggs there, and raised their young. We were careful not to go near them in the summer, of course—that's the breeding season. And there is another mystery—for there are no seasons under the sea. But the saurians remembered. . . .

It was dangerous.

"But not as dangerous as what Maeva did for me two months ago.

"She found me in Joe Trencher's sea car. She brought the edenite cylinder from my father, along with a message. And she helped me get away in the sea car.

"Trencher followed—naturally. I don't know if he suspected her or not. I hope not." David's face looked pinched and drawn as he said it.

"Anyway," he went on, "Joe Trencher followed me—not in a sea car, but swimming free, and riding one of the saurians. They can make a fabulous rate of speed in the open sea—they kept right after me. And then they caught me."

David looked up.

"And the rest you know," he said. "Now—it's up to all of us. And we don't have much time."

We didn't have much time.

But time passed.

David went back to the little apartment over the boat shed, to wait. Roger and Bob and I went on with our classes.

The next day there was not much time for thinking. It was only a week until Graduation Week, and there were the last of our examinations to get through. Hard to focus our minds on Mahan's theories and the physics of liquid masses, with high adventure in the background! But we had to do it.

And after the final day of examinations, no break. For there was close-order drill, parade formation. We struggled into our dress-scarlet uniforms and fell out for unending hours of countermarching and wheeling. It wasn't our own graduation we would be marching for—but every one of us looked forward to the time when we would be sworn in before the assembled ranks of the Academy, and every one of us clipped off the maneuvers with every ounce of precision we could manage. It was blistering hot in the Bermuda sun as we practiced, hour after hour, for the final review. Then, just before the sunset gun, there came a welcome change. The cumulus masses had been building and towering over the sea; they came lowering in on us, split with lightning flashes. The clouds opened up, and pelting rain drenched us all.

We raced for shelter, any shelter we could find.

I found myself in the lee of an upended whaleboat, and crouched beside me was another cadet, as wet as I. He brushed rivulets of rain from his flat-visored dress-scarlet cap and turned to me, grinning.

It was Eladio Angel.

"Jim!" he cried. "Jim Eden! So long since I have seen you!"

I took his hand as he held it out to shake, and I suppose I must have said something. But I don't know what.

Eladio Angel—David Craken's old roommate, his close friend, the only cadet in all the Academy, save Bob Eskow and myself, who thought enough of David to feel the loss when he was gone.

And what could I say to Laddy Angel now?

He was going on and on. "—since you wrote your letter to Jason Craken, the father of David. Ah, David—even now, Jim, I think sometimes of him. So great a loss, so good a friend! I can scarcely believe that he is gone. And truly, Jim, even to this day I cannot believe it. No, in my heart I believe he is alive somewhere—somehow he escaped, somehow he did not drown. But—enough!" He grinned again. "Tell me, Jim, how are you? I have seen you only a time or two, leaving a class or crossing the quadrangle—we have not had time to speak. Convenient, this rain—it causes us to meet again!"

I cleared my throat. "Why—why, yes, Laddy," I said, uncomfortably. "Yes, it—it certainly is good to see you again. I, uh——" I pretended to look out at the teeming rain and to be surprised. "Why, look, Laddy!" I cried. "I believe it's letting up! Well, I've got to get back to dorm—I'll be seeing you!"

And I fled, through the unrelenting downpour.

I could feel his eyes on my back as I went—not angry, but hurt. Undoubtedly hurt. I had been rude to him—but what could I do? David had said, over and over, that we must keep this matter secret—and I am no accomplished liar, that I could talk to his close friend and not give away the secret that he was not dead!

But I didn't have much time to brood about it. As I was racing across the quadrangle, drenched to the skin, someone hailed me. "Eden! Cadet Eden, report!"

I skidded to a halt and saluted.

It was an upperclassman, on temporary duty with the Commandant's office. He was outfitted in bad-weather oilskins, only his face peeping out into the downpour. He returned my salute uncomfortably, rain pouring into his sleeve as he lifted his arm.

"Cadet Eden," he rapped, "report to the Commandant's office immediately! Someone to see you!"

Someone to see me?

The standing orders of the Academy are: *Cadets reporting to the Commandant will do so on the double!* But I didn't need the spur of the standing orders to make me move. I could hardly wait to get there—for I could not imagine who might want me. If it was David, or anyone connected with David, it could only mean trouble. Bad trouble, bad enough to make him give up his secrecy. . . .

But it wasn't trouble at all.

I ran panting into the Commandant's outer office and braked to stiff attention. Even while I was saluting I gasped: "Cadet Eden, sir, reporting as ordered by——"

I stopped, astonished.

A tall, black figure was getting up out of a chair in the reception room—a figure I knew well, the figure of someone I had thought to be half a world away. Gideon Park!

He grinned at me, his white teeth flashing. "Jim," he said, in his soft, mild voice. "Your uncle said you needed help. Here I am!"

11

Graduation Week

Gideon Park! Tall, black, loyal—just to see him there waiting for me in the Commandant's office took an enormous weight off my shoulders. Gideon and I had been in plenty of tight spots together, and I had a lot of respect for the man.

Maybe we had a chance to carry through our plans after all!

Gideon and I had only a moment to talk together, that first afternoon. I whispered to him where he could find David Craken—in the boathouse on the estate of Trident's Atlantic manager. He nodded and winked and left.

And I went back to dorm to get ready for evening mess, feeling better than I had in days.

I couldn't get off Academy grounds that evening, but Bob hadn't used all his passes. Right after evening chow he took off for the boathouse, to talk things over with Gideon and David Craken.

He returned seconds before Lights Out. He had been gone nearly four hours.

"It's all right," he whispered to me, hastily getting ready for bed. "Gideon brought the money with him."

"How much?" I asked, keeping my own voice down—if the duty officer heard us, it was a demerit. And it was too close to the end of the school year to want demerits.

"Enough. Ninety-seven thousand dollars, Jim! He had it with him in cash. That's the most money I ever saw in one place."

I nodded in the darkness. "Ninety-seven thousand," I repeated. "Funny amount—I suppose it was every penny he could raise." It was a grim thought. I whispered urgently: "Bob, we've got to come through on this! If I know my uncle, he's gone in debt for this—he's repaying an obligation to Jason Craken. If anything goes wrong—if we can't help Craken, can't get this money back for my uncle—it'll mean trouble for him."

"Of course, Jim." Bob was in bed already. "Gideon's going to Sargasso Dome tomorrow," he whispered. "To put up the bond so that our bid will be counted. There isn't much time left."

"Did you tell David that I'd seen Laddy Angel?"

There was a pause for a second. "I—I forgot, Jim. I didn't have much time, anyway. I was only there for a few minutes——"

I sat straight up in bed. "Only a few minutes! But, Bob—you were gone for hours!"

His voice was apologetic—and strained. "I was, well, delayed, Jim. I, uh——"

We both heard the rapping of the duty officer's heels in the corridor outside.

That put an end to the conversation. But I couldn't help wondering fuzzily, as I went to sleep—if Bob was gone four hours, and had only a few minutes in the beach house . . . what had he done with the rest of his time?

"Atten-HUT!"

The voice of the Commandant roared through the loudhailers, and the whole student body of the Academy snapped to.

"By squadrons! Forward MARCH!"

The sea band struck up the Academy anthem, and the classes passed in review.

It was the end of Graduation Week. We wheeled briskly off the Quadrangle, past the reviewing stands, down the crushed coral of the Ramp, to the dispersal areas.

The school year was at an end.

Bob Eskow and I were now upperclassmen, with the whole summer ahead of us.

And today was the day when the sealed bids of the condemned Fleet cruisers would be opened—and we would know if we owned the *Killer Whale* or not.

Bob and I raced back to barracks. Discipline was at an end! The halls were full of milling cadets, talking, laughing, making plans for the summer. Even the duty officers, for once relaxed and smiling, were walking around, shaking hands with the cadets they had been dressing down or putting on report a few hours before.

We quickly changed into off-duty whites and headed

toward the gate. The guards were still stiffly formal, at ramrod attention; but as we automatically braked to a halt in front of the guardbox and reached instinctively for the passes that we didn't have, one of them unbent and grinned. "You're on your own time now, cadets!" he murmured. "Have a good time!"

We nodded and walked past——

But not very far.

"Bob Eskow! Jim!"

A voice crying our names, behind us. We turned, but even before I looked I knew who it was.

Eladio Angel! His face was serious and determined. He was trotting to catch up with us.

Bob and I looked at each other as he came toward us, his dark eyes serious, his mouth grim. In all these months we had hardly spoken to him, barring the one time I had met him under the boat hull and had left him so abruptly.

And now—just when we could least afford to have him with us, here he was!

He stopped in front of us, panting slightly.

"Jim," he said sharply. "Come, I am going with you."

"With us? But—but, Laddy——"

He shook his head. "No, Jim. It is no use to argue with me. I have thought, and I am not wrong." He smiled faintly, seriously. "I ask myself, why should Jim Eden be rude? There is no answer, for you are not the sort who does this. No answer—unless there is something you do not wish to tell me. So I wait there, Jim," he said earnestly, looking into my eyes. "I wait there under the boat, where you have left me. And I look at the rain which is coming down by torrents and buckets, Jim, the rain which you have said is almost over. And I say: 'Jim Eden has one secret.' What can this secret be? Ah, there is only one answer, for I have noticed the look on your face when I mention a certain name. So I ask questions, and I find you have been going off grounds much of the time. Many times. And always to the same place—and there is someone there you visit, someone no one sees.

"So—the secret is no secret, Jim, for I have figured it out." He grinned openly, with friendly warmth. "So let us go then, Jim," he said, "all three of us—let us go to see my friend who is not lost, my friend you have been visiting by stealth—David Craken!"

The electronic beam leaped out, coral-pink in the afternoon daylight, and scanned my face. "You may enter," rapped out the voice from the watchman-machine, and the doors wavered slightly and relaxed.

We walked through the fairy garden, following the palely glimmering Troyon lights that marked the path we were permitted to take. Since the watchman had been repaired there had been no other trouble. But of course, the one time was enough.

We came to a crossing and Laddy absentmindedly started to take a wrong turning, down a shell-pink lane toward a fountain that began to play as we came near it. At once the coral scanning ray leaped from a hidden viewport, and the mechanical voice squawked: "Go back, go back! You are not permitted! Go back!"

I caught Laddy Angel by the shoulder and steered him onto the right path. It wasn't entirely safe to disobey the orders of the electronic watchman. It had its weapons against intruders—true, it was not likely to shoot Laddy down, merely for stepping on the wrong path; but there was the chance it might transmit an alarm to the Police headquarters in Hamilton if its electronic brain thought there was danger to its master's property. And we still didn't want the publicity the police might bring.

"Funny," said Bob Eskow from behind me.

"What's funny?"

"Well——" he hesitated. "Roger Fairfane. He talks so much about how important his father is, and how he has the run of Trident Lines. And yet here he's restricted to the boathouse. Doesn't it seem funny to you, Jim? I mean, if his father is such a hot-shot, wouldn't the Atlantic manager of his father's line let Roger have the run of the whole place?"

I shrugged. "Let's not worry about it," I said. "Laddy, here we are. David is waiting in the apartment there, above the boat basin."

I had been a little worried—worried that David would be angry because we'd brought Laddy along.

But I needn't have worried. It took two or three words

of explanation, and then he was grinning. He shrugged. "You're quite a detective, Laddy," he conceded. "To tell you the truth—I'm glad you figured it out. It's good to see you!"

Gideon hadn't returned from Sargasso City yet, and there wasn't much to do until he did. So the four of us—five when Roger showed up, half an hour or so later—spent the next couple of hours talking over old times. David had food ready in the automatic kitchen; we ate a good meal, watched a baseball game on the stereovision set in the living room, and just loafed.

It was the most relaxing afternoon I had spent in a long time.

Unfortunately, it didn't last.

It was getting late when we heard the distant rattle of the gate loudspeaker challenging someone and, a moment later, I saw from the window the tiny violet sparks of the Troyon lights marking the pathway for the visitor.

"Must be Gideon," I cried. "He's coming this way. I hope he's got good news!"

It was Gideon, all right. He came in; but he didn't get any farther than the door before all five of us were leaping at him, firing questions. "Did we get it? Come on, Gideon—don't keep us waiting! What's the story? Did we get the *Killer Whale?*"

He looked at us all silently for a moment.

The questions stopped. Every one of us realized that something was wrong in the same second. We stood there, frozen, waiting for him to speak.

He said at last: "Jim, did you say you saw this Joe Trencher in Sargasso City when you put in the bid?"

"Why—why, yes, Gideon. He was poking around the papers, but I don't think he——"

"You think wrong, Jim." Gideon's black, strong face was bleak. His soft voice had a touch of anger to it that I had seldom heard. "Do you remember anything else about that day?"

"Well—let me think." I tried to think back. "We went down to the Fleet basin. There were the ships that were up for surplus—the *Killer* and that other one, the heap of rust. The *Dolphin*. We looked the *Killer* over and filled out the forms. Then, while I was calling my uncle, Joe

Trencher started poking around the papers. And—well, we couldn't catch him. So we just filed the bid applications and caught the sub-sea shuttle back here."

Gideon nodded somberly.

David cried: "Gideon, what's wrong? I've got to have that cruiser! It's—it's my father's life that's at stake. If we didn't bid enough—well, then maybe we can raise some more money, somehow. But I must have it!"

"Oh, the bid was enough," said Gideon. "But——"

"But what, Gideon?"

He sighed. "I guess Joe Trencher knew what he was doing," he said, in that soft, chuckling voice, now sounding worried. "He put in a bid himself, you see."

It was bad news.

We looked at each other. David said at last, his voice hoarse and ragged: "Joe Trencher. With the pearls he stole from me, he bought the ship I need to save my father's life. And there's no time now to go back and try something else. It's almost time——"

Time for what, I wondered—but Roger Fairfane interrupted him. "Is that it, Gideon?" he demanded. "Did Trencher make a higher bid, so that we don't have a ship?"

Gideon shook his head.

"Not exactly," he said. "Trencher owns the *Killer Whale* now, but he got it for fifty thousand dollars—the same as you bid."

"But—but then what——"

"You see," said Gideon gently, "Trencher wasn't just looking at those papers. He—changed them. Changed them his way. I made the Fleet commander show them to me, and it was obvious that they'd been changed—but of course I couldn't prove anything." He looked at us somberly. "The ship you bid on wasn't the *Killer Whale*," he said. "Not after Trencher got through with the papers. What you bid on—and what you now own—is the other one. The heap of rust, as you called it, Jim. The *Dolphin*."

12

Rustbucket Navy

The next day David Craken and I went to Sargasso City to pick up our prize.

The *Killer Whale* still lay in the slip beside it. Obsolescent, no doubt—but sleek and deadly as the sea beast for which she was named. She lay low in the water, her edenite hull rippling with pale light where the wavelets washed against it.

Next to the *Killer,* our *Dolphin* looked like the wreck she was.

Naturally, there was no sign of Joe Trencher. For a moment I had the wild notion of waiting there—keeping a watch on the *Killer Whale,* laying in wait until Trencher came to claim the ship he had cheated us out of and then confronting him. . . .

But what good would it have done? And besides, there was no time. David had said several times that we had only a few weeks. In July something was going to happen—something that he was mysterious about, but something that was dangerous.

It was now the beginning of June. We had at the most four weeks to refit the *Dolphin,* get under weigh, make the long voyage down under the Americas, around the Horn (for we had to avoid the Fleet inspection that would come if we went through the Canal)—and help David's father.

It was a big job. . . .

And the *Dolphin* was a very small ship.

David looked at me and grinned wryly. "Well," he said, "let's go aboard."

The *Dolphin* had been a fine and famous ship—thirty years before.

We picked our way through a tangle of discarded gear—evidently her last crew had been so happy to get off her that they hadn't waited to pack!

We found ourselves in her wardroom. The tarnished

brass tablets welded to the bulkhead recorded the high moments of her history. We paused to read them.

In spite of everything, I couldn't help feeling a thrill.

She had held the speed and depth records for her class for three solid years.

She had been the flagship of Admiral Kane—back before I was born, on his Polar expeditions, when he sonargraphed the sea floor under the ice.

She had hunted down and sunk the subsea pirate who used the name Davy Jones.

And later—still seaworthy, but too old for regular service with the Fleet—she had become a training ship at the Academy. She'd been salvaged two or three years back, just before any of us had come to the Academy, and finally put up for auction.

And now she was ours.

We took a room for the night in one of Sargasso Dome's hotels. It was a luxurious place, full of pleasures for vacationers and tourists anxious to sample the imitation mysteries of the fabled Sargasso Sea. But we were in no mood to enjoy it. We went to bed and lay awake for a long time, both of us, wondering if the *Dolphin's* ancient armor would survive the crushing pressures of the Deeps. . . .

Roger Fairfane shook us awake.

I sat up, blinking, and glanced at my wrist-chronometer.

It was only about five o'clock in the morning. I said blurrily, "Roger! What—what are you doing here? I thought you were still in Bermuda."

"I was." He was scowling worriedly. "We had to come right away—all of us. Laddy's with me, and Bob and Gideon. We took the night shuttle from Bermuda."

David was out of his bed, standing beside us. "What's the matter, Roger?"

"Plenty! It's that Joe Trencher again! The bid he made on the *Dolphin*—it was in the name of something called the Sub-Sea Salvage Corporation. Well, somebody checked into the sale of surplus ships—and they found that no such firm existed. Gideon found out that an order is going to be issued at nine o'clock this morning, canceling all sales.

"So—if we want to use the *Dolphin* to help your father, David, we've got to get under weigh before the order comes through at nine!"

It didn't give us much time!

David and I had looked forward to at least a full day's testing of the *Dolphin's* old propulsion and pressure equipment. Even then, it would have been dangerous enough, taking the old ship out into the crushing pressures that surrounded Sargasso Dome.

But now we had only hours!

"Well—thank heaven we've got help," muttered David as we dressed hurriedly and checked out of the hotel. "I'm glad Gideon flew in from Marinia! And Laddy. We'll need every one of us, to keep that old tub of rust afloat!"

"I only hope that's enough to do it," I grumbled. We raced after Roger Fairfane, down the corridors, through the passenger elevators, to the sea-floor levels where the *Dolphin* and the *Killer Whale* floated quietly. . . .

"It's gone!" cried Dave as we came onto the catwalk over the basin. "The *Killer's* gone!"

"Sure it is," said Roger. "Didn't I tell you? Trencher must have heard too—the *Killer* was already gone when we got here. Isn't that the payoff?" he went on disgustedly. "Trencher's the one that caused all this trouble—but he's got away already with the *Killer* "

Gideon was already at work, checking the edenite armor film, his face worried. He looked up as we trotted up the gangplank to the above-decks hatch.

"Think she'll stand pressure, Gideon?" I asked him.

He pushed back his hat and stared at the rippling line of light where the little wavelets licked the *Dolphin's* side.

"Think so?" he repeated. "No, Jim. I'll tell you the truth. I don't think so. Not from anything I can see. She ought to be towed out and scuttled, from what I see. Her edenite film's defective—it'll need a hundred-hour job of repair on the generators before I can really trust it. Her power plant is ten years overdue for salvage. One of her pumps is broken down. And the whole power plant, pumps and all, is hot with leaded radiation. If I had my way, I'd scrap the whole plant down to the bedplates."

I stared at him. "But—but, Gideon———"

He held up his hand. "All the same, Jim," he went on, in his soft voice, "she floats. And I've talked to the salvage officer here—got him out of bed to do it—and she came in on her own power, with her own armor keeping the sea out. Well, that was only a month ago. If she could do it then, she can do it now."

He grinned. "These subsea vessels," he said, "they aren't just piles of machinery. They live! This one looks like it's fit for the junkyard and nothing else—but it's still running, and as long as she's running, I'll take my chances in her!"

"That's good enough for me!" David said promptly.

"I'll go along with that," I told them. "How about Laddy and Bob?"

"They're belowdecks already," Gideon said. "Trying to get the engines turning over. Hear that?"

We all listened.

No, we didn't hear anything—at least I didn't. But I could *feel* something. Down in the soles of my feet, where they touched the rounded upper hump of the *Dolphin's* armor, I could feel a faint, low vibration.

The ship was alive! That vibration was the old engines, turning over at last!

Gideon said, "That's it, Jim. We can push off as soon as they'll open the sea-gates for us." He turned to Roger Fairfane. "You're the only one who hasn't expressed himself. What about it? You want to come along—or do you think it's too dangerous?"

Roger scowled nervously. "I—I———" he began.

Then he grinned. "I'm coming!" he told us. "Not only that—but remember our ranks! I'm the senior cadet officer of the whole lot of us—and Gideon and David aren't even cadets, much less officers. So I'm the captain, remember!"

The captain nearly had a mutiny on his hands in the first five minutes.

But Gideon calmed us down.

"What's the difference?" he asked us, in his soft, serious voice. "Let him be captain. We've got to have one, don't we? And we're all pulling together. . . ."

"I don't know if *he* is," grumbled Bob. We were in the old wardroom, stowing our navigation charts away, waiting for the Fleet officer to give us clearance to go through the shiplocks into the open sea. "But—I guess you're right. He's the captain, if he wants it that way. *I* don't care. . . ."

There was a rattle and blare from abovedecks. We leaped out of the wardroom to listen.

"Ahoy, vessel *Dolphin!*" a voice came roaring through the loudhailers of the Fleet office. "You are cleared for Lock Baker. Good voyage!"

"Thank you!" cried Roger Fairfane's voice, through the loudspeakers from the bridge. We heard the rattle of the warning system, and the creaking, moaning sound of the engines dogging down the hatch.

We all ran to our stations—doublemanning them for this first venture into the depths.

My station was at the bridge, by Roger Fairfane's side. He signaled to Laddy Angel and Bob Eskow, down at the engines, for dead slow speed ahead.

Inch by inch, on the microsonar charts before us, we saw the little green pip that marked the *Dolphin* crawl in to Lock Baker.

We stopped engines as the nose of the ship nuzzled into the cradle of rope bumpers.

The lock gates closed behind us.

The *Dolphin* pitched sharply and rolled as high-pressure sea water jetted into the lock from the deep sea outside.

I could hear the whine of the edenite field generator rise a whole octave as it took the force of all that enormous pressure and turned it back upon itself, guarding us against the frightful squeeze.

The hull of the old ship sparkled and coruscated with green fire as the pressure hit it.

The lock door opened before us.

Roger Fairfane rang *Dead Slow Ahead* on the engine telegraph.

And our ship moved out into the punishing sea.

I suppose it was luck that kept us alive.

Gideon came pounding up from the engine room. "Set

course for the surface!" he cried. "She's an old ship, Roger, and the edenite field isn't what it should be. Bring her up boy, bring her up! She's taking water!"

Roger flushed and seemed about to challenge Gideon—after all, Roger was the captain! But there was no arguing with the pressure of the deeps. He flipped the fore and aft diving fanes into full climb, rang *Flank Speed* on the telegraph.

The old *Dolphin* twisted and surged ahead.

I raced down the companionways with Gideon to check the leaks.

They weren't too bad—but any leak is bad, when two miles of water lie over your head. There was just a feather of spray, leaping out where two plates joined and the edenite field didn't quite fill the gap between. "I can fix them, Jim," Gideon said, half to himself. "We'll cruise on the surface, and I'll strip down the edenite generator and the hull will hold—— Only let's get up topside now!"

It was two miles to go.

But the old *Dolphin* made it.

We porpoised to the surface—bad seamanship, that was, but we were in a hurry. And then we set course, south by east, for the long, long swing around the Cape into the South Pacific. On the surface we couldn't make our full rated speed—unlike the old submarines, the *Dolphin* was designed to stay underwater; its plump, stubby silhouette was for underwater performance, and cruising on the surface was actually harder for it. But we could make pretty good time all the same.

And Gideon set to work at once to strip down the old generators. We could get by with the steel plates that underlay the edenite field—as long as we stayed on the surface. And once Gideon had finished his job, we could get back into the deeps where we belonged. There we would churn off the long miles to Tonga Deep. It was halfway around the world, and a bit more—for the long detour around South America added thousands of miles to our trip. At forty knots—and Gideon promised us forty knots—we would be over Tonga Trench in just about two weeks.

David Craken and I checked our position with a solar

fix and laid out our course on the navigator's charts. "Two weeks," I said, and he nodded.

"Two weeks." He stared bleakly into space. "I only hope we're in time——"

"Craken! Eden!"

Roger's voice came, shrill with excitement, from the bridge. We jumped out of the navigator's cubbyhole to join him.

"Look at that!" he commanded, pointing to the microsonar. "What do you make of it?"

I stared at the screen. There was a tiny blob of light— behind us and well below. At least a hundred fathoms down.

I tried to get a closer scan by narrowing the field. It made the tiny blob a shade brighter, a fraction clearer. . . .

"There it is!" cried Roger Fairfane, and there was an edge of panic in his voice now.

I couldn't blame him.

For the image in the microsonar was, for a split second, clear and bright.

Then it became a blob again and dwindled; but in that moment I had seen a strange silhouette. A ship?

Maybe. But if it was a ship, it was a queer one. A fantastic one—for it had a strange conning tower, shaped like a great triangular head, on a long, twisting neck!

I turned to David Craken, a question on my lips.

I didn't have to ask it.

His face was pale as he nodded. "That's right, Jim," he said. "It's a saurian. A—sea serpent. And it's on our trail."

13

The Followers of the Deeps

It dogged us endlessly—for hour after unending hour, day after day.

By and by we became used to it, and we could even joke; but it was a joke with a current of worry running close beneath. For there was no doubt that the saurian that followed was in some way closely related to Joe Trencher—to the *Killer Whale*—and to the amphibian revolt against David Craken's father.

We crossed the Equator—and had a little ceremony, like the sailing men of old, initiating the lubbers into the mysteries of Davy Jones. But there was only one lubber among us. Gideon and David Craken had crossed the Equator many times beyond counting—Laddy Angel's home, after all, was in Peru—and even Bob and I had made the long trip to Marinia one time before.

Roger was our lubber—and, surprisingly, he took the nonsense initiation in good part. Drenched with a ship's bucket of icy salt water from the pressure lock (for we were running submerged once more, the edenite film glistening quietly on our plates), choking with laughter, he cried: "Have your fun, boys! Once this is over, I'll be the captain again—and I have a long memory!"

But it was a joke, not a threat—and I found myself liking Roger Fairfane for almost the first time since we had met.

But once the initiation was over, and he had come out of his cabin in dry clothes, he was withdrawn and reserved again.

We put in at a little port on the bulge of Brazil for the stores we had been unable to load in Sargasso Dome. There was money to spare for everything we needed—for everything but one thing. Gideon went ashore and stayed for hours, and came back looking drawn and worried. "Nothing doing," he reported. "I tried, Jim, believe me I tried. I even went down to the dives along the waterfront and tried to make a contact. But there's no armament to be had. We've got a fighting ship, but we've nothing to fight with. And there's no chance now that we'll get guns for it."

David Craken listened and nodded soberly. "It's all right," he told us. "I knew we'd have trouble getting guns—the Fleet doesn't sell its vessels with armaments, and they make it pretty hard for anyone to get them. But my father—he has weapons, in his dome. If we can get there——"

He left it unfinished.

We drove along through waters that began to show the traces of the melted glaciers of Antarctica. A fraction denser, a part of a degree cooler, a few parts less per million of salt—we were nearing the tip of the South American continent.

We slipped through the Straits one dark night, running submerged, feeling our way by sonar and by chart. It was a tricky passage—but there was a Fleet base on Terra del Fuego, and we wanted to avoid attention.

Once we were in the Pacific all of us, by common impulse, leaped for the microsonar to see if our implacable follower had navigated the Straits right after us.

It had.

The tiny blob that sometimes drew close enough to show a three-cornered head and a ropy neck—it was still following, still there.

It was still there as we breasted the Peru Current and struck out into the Pacific itself.

Laddy Angel looked at the sounding instruments with a wry expression. "Cold and fast—it is the Peru Current. Odd, but it causes me to feel almost homesick!"

Roger Fairfane, off duty but lounging around the bridge laughed sharply. "Homesick? For a current in the ocean?"

Laddy drew up his eyebrows. "Ah, you laugh, my captain. But trust me, the Peru Current is indeed Peru. Some years it fails—it is a fickle current, and perhaps it wanders out to sea for a few months, to try if it likes the deep sea better than the land. Those years are bad years for my country. For the Current brings food; the food brings little creatures for the sea-birds to feed upon; the sea-birds make guano and themselves make food for bigger fish. And on these things my country must depend." He nodded soberly. "Laugh at a current in the ocean if you wish to, but to my country it is life."

The *Dolphin* pounded on. Past the longitude of the Galapagos, past strange old Easter Island. We stayed clear of land; actually we were not close to anything but the sea bottom, but each time we passed the longitude of an island or island group, David Craken marked it off with his neat pencil tick, and checked the calendar, and sighed. Time was passing.

And the saurian hung on behind.

Sometimes it seemed as though there were two of them. Sometimes the little blob behind us seemed to be joined by another, smaller. I asked David: "Can it be two sea serpents? Do they travel in pairs?"

He shrugged, but there was an expression of worry in his eyes. "They travel sometimes in huge herds, Jim. But that other thing—I don't think it is a saurian."

"What then?"

He shook his head. "If it is what I think," he said soberly, "we'll find out soon enough. If not, there is no point in worrying."

Gideon, head deep in the complex entrails of the old fire-control monitor, looked up from his job of repair. It was a low-priority job, because we had no armament to fire; but Gideon had made it his business to get everything in readiness for the moment when we might reach Jason Craken's sub-sea dome. If we could ship arms there, we would have the fire-control monitor in working shape to handle them. He had checked everything—from the escape capsule in the keelson to the microsonars at the bridge.

He said softly: "David. We've less than a thousand miles to go. Don't you think it's time you took us all the way into your confidence?"

"About what?"

"Why, David, about those saurians, as you call them. Jim says you've told him something about them, but I must say there are things I don't understand."

David hesitated. He had the conn, but there was in truth little for him to do. The *Dolphin* was cruising at 5500 feet on the robot pilot—the proper level for westbound traffic in that part of the Pacific. The indicators showed that the edenite pressure system was working perfectly; there was no water sloshing about the bilge, no warning blare of horns to show a hull failure, or fission products leaking from the old engines. We were cruising fast and dry.

David glanced at the microsonar, where the tiny, remorseless pip hung on behind.

Then he took a folded chart from his locker and spread it before us.

All of us gathered around—Gideon and Bob and Laddy and Roger and I. The chart was marked *Tonga Trench*—a standard Fleet survey chart, but with many details penciled in where the Fleet's survey ships had left white banks. There was the long, bare furrow of the Trench itself—more than a thousand miles, end to end.

And someone—David or his father, I supposed—had penciled in a cluster of sea-mounts and chasms, with current arrows and soundings.

David placed his finger on one of the sea-mounts.

"There," he said. "There's something that many men would give a million dollars to know. That's where the Tonga pearls come from."

I heard Roger make a strange, excited gasping sound beside me.

"And there," David went on, "is the birthplace of the saurians. Great sea reptiles! My father says they are the descendants of the creatures that ruled the seas a hundred million years ago and more. Plesiosaurs, he says. They disappeared from the face of the deep, millions and millions of years before Man came along.

"But not all of them. Down in the Tonga Trench, some of them lived on."

He folded the chart again jealously, as though he was afraid we would memorize it. "They attacked my father's sea-car, forty years ago, when he first tried to dive into the Tonga Trench. He beat them off and got away with the first Tonga pearls that ever saw the light of day—but he never forgot them. Since then, he's been studying them. Trying to domesticate them, even—with the help of the amphibians, partly, and partly by raising some of them from captured eggs. But they aren't very intelligent, really, and they are very hard to train.

"You've heard the old mariners' stories about sea-serpents? My father says these saurians are behind the stories. Once or twice a century, he says, a young male would be driven out of the herds, and roam about the world, looking for mates. They avoid the surfaces most of the time—the lack of pressure is painful to them—but a few of them have been seen. And they have never been forgotten. Big as whales, scaled, with long necks. They swim with enormous paddle-limbs. They must have terrified the windjammers—they were bigger than some of the ships!"

Bob Eskow frowned. "I've heard of the Plesiosaurs," he said. "They're descended from reptiles that once lived on dry land—like all the big sea saurians. And that thing that's following us, is that one of them?"

David nodded. "One of the tamed ones. The amphibians work them. Joe Trencher is using them in his rebellion against my father."

The *Dolphin* pounded on, through the deep, dark seas. David Craken looked up finally from his charts. His face was clouded. He said "We're a long way off the main sea routes. It's been a long time since we passed a sonar beacon for a fix. But—I think we are . . . here."

His finger stabbed a tiny penciled cross on the chart.

The Tonga Trench!

His expression cleared and he grinned at Roger. "Captain Fairfane," he reported formally, "I have a course correction for you. Azimuth, steady on two twenty-five degrees. Elevation, negative five degrees." He grinned and translated. "Straight ahead and down!"

Gideon said soberly: "Just a few more hours then, David. Are we in time?"

David Craken shrugged. "I hope so. I think so."

He looked at the sonarscope, where the tiny little blob that was the pursuing saurian hung on. He said: "You see, it is almost July—and July is the month of breeding for them. My father—he's a willful man, Gideon. He chose to build his dome on a little mound on the slope of a sea-mount, and he must have known long before the work was finished that it was a bad place. Because it is there that the saurians go to lay their eggs. They come up out of the Trench—Dad says it is a pattern of behavior that dates back hundreds of millions of years, perhaps to the time when they still went to the beaches on dry land, as turtles sometimes do today.

"Anyway—Dad's dome is directly in their path." David shook his head broodingly. "While he was well, while he had the amphibians to help him—he managed to fight them off, and I believe he enjoyed it. But now he's sick, and alone, and the amphibians are bound to try something at the same time. . . ."

He glanced again at the scope of the microsonar.

"Gideon!" he cried. "Jim!"

We clustered around, staring.

There was another blob of light there once more—the featured little speck that was the saurian, and the other tiny one that hung around it.

But it was larger than ever before.

Even as we watched it grew larger and larger.

Gideon said, frowning, "Something's coming mighty fast. Another saurian? But it's faster than the other one has ever gone. It's gaining on us as though we were floating still. . . ."

David's face was drained of color.

He said lifelessly: "It isn't a saurian, Gideon."

Roger and Laddy and Bob were talking, all at once. I elbowed my way past them to get to the ranging dials of the microsonar. The little blips grew fuzzy, then sharper, then fuzzy once more. I cried: "Please! Give me room!"

I turned again to the dials and gently coaxed the images back. They grew brighter, sharper. . . .

"You're right, David!" Gideon's voice was soft and worried behind me. "That's no saurian!"

It was a sea-car—a big one. Bigger than ours.

I cracked the range dial a hairs-breadth.

The image leaped into clear focus.

The shape in the microsonar was the sleek and deadly outline of the *Killer Whale!*

14

Sub-Sea Skirmish

The ship was the *Killer*, no question about it.

It was headed straight for us. Roger looked around at the rest of us, his face pale. "Well what about it?" he demanded. "What can they do? They've no armament, have they? The Fleet must have stripped the *Killer* just as they did the *Dolphin*——"

"Don't count on it," David said quietly. "Remember, Trencher's at home under the water. They've been delayed for something—they must have put the saurian to following us, while they were doing something. Doing what? I don't know, Roger. But I could make a guess, and my guess would be that they've been stripping sunken ships somewhere, taking armament off them. . . . I don't know, I admit. But if you think they can hurt us, Roger, I'm afraid you're living in a fool's paradise."

Roger said harshly: "Eden! Give them a hail on the sonarphone! Ask them what they want."

"Aye-aye, sir!" I started the sonarphone pulsing and beamed a message at the ship behind us. *"Dolphin to Killer Whale. Dolphin to Killer Whale!"*

No answer.

I tried again: *"Dolphin to Killer Whale! Come in, Killer Whale."*

Silence, while we waited. The sonarphone picked up and amplified the noises of the ship behind us, the half-musical whine of her atomic turbines, the soft hissing of the water sliding past her edenite armor.

But there was no answer.

Roger glared at me and shouldered past. He picked up the sonarphone mike himself. *"Killer Whale!"* he cried. "This is the *Dolphin*, Roger Fairfane commanding. I demand you answer——"

I stopped listening abruptly.

I had glanced at the microsonar screen. Against the dark field that was black sea water, I saw a bright little fleck dart away from the bright silhouette of the *Killer*.

I leaped past Roger to the autopilot, cut it out with a flick of the switch, grabbed the conn wheel and heaved the *Dolphin* into a crash dive.

Everyone went sprawling and clinging to whatever they could hold. Roger Fairfane fought his way up, glaring at me, his face contorted. "Eden! I'm in command here! If you—"

Whump.

A dull concussion interrupted him. The old *Dolphin*

shook and shivered, and the strained metal of her hull made ominous snapping sounds.

"What was that?" Roger cried.

Gideon answered. "A jet missile," he said. "If Jim hadn't crash-dived us—we'd be trying to breathe water right now."

Cut and run!

We jumped to battle stations, and Roger poured on the coal.

Battle stations. But what did we have to fight with? The *Killer Whale* had found arms somewhere—either by salvaging wrecks or buying them in some illegal way. But we had none.

Bob Eskow and Gideon manned the engines, and coaxed every watt of power out of the creaking old reactors.

It wasn't enough. Newer, bigger, faster—the *Killer Whale* was gaining on us. Roger, sweating, banged the handle of the engine-room telegraph uselessly against the stops. He grabbed the speaking tube and cried: "Engine room! Eskow, listen. Cut out the safety stops—run the reactors on manual. We'll need more power!"

Bob's voice rattled back, with a note of alarm: "On manual? But Roger—these reactors are old! If we cut out the safety stops——"

"That's an order!" blazed Roger, and slammed the microphone into its cradle. He looked anxiously to me, manning the microsonar. "Are we gaining, Eden?"

I shook my head. "No, sir. They're still closing up. I—I guess they're trying to get so close that we can't dodge their missiles."

Beside me, David Craken was working the fathometer, tracing our course on the chart he had made. He looked up, and he was almost smiling. "Roger—Jim!" he cried. "I—I think we're going to make it." He stabbed at the chart with his pencil. "The last sounding shows we've just passed a check point. It isn't more than twenty miles to my father's sea-mount!"

I stared over his shoulder. The little pencil tick he had made showed us well over the slope of the Tonga Trench. There was thirty thousand feet of water from the surface to the muck at the bottom, and we were nearly halfway between. The long, crooked outline of the Tonga and Kermadec Trenches sprawled a thousand miles across the great chart on the bulkhead—went completely off the little chart David was using. We were over the cliffs at the brink of the great, strange furrow itself, heading steeply down.

I caught myself and glanced at the microsonar screen—just barely in time. "Missile! Take evasive action!"

Roger wrestled the conn wheel over and down; the old *Dolphin* went into a spiraling, descending turn.

Whump.

It was closer than before.

Roger panted something indistinguishable and grabbed the microphone again. "Bob! I've got to have more power!"

It was Gideon who answered this time. Even now, his voice was soft and gentle. "I'm afraid we don't have any more power to give, Roger. The reactor's overheating now."

"But I've *got* to have more power!"

Gideon said softly: "There's something leaking inside the shield. I guess the old conduits were pretty badly corroded—that last missile may have sprung them." The gentle voice paused for a second. Then it went on: "We've been trying to keep it running, but you don't repair Series K reactors, Roger. It's hot now. Way past the red line. If it gets any hotter, we'll have to dump it—or else abandon ship!"

For a while I thought we might make it.

At full power, the old *Dolphin* was eating up the last few miles to Jason Craken's sea-mount and the dome. Even the *Killer Whale*, bigger and newer and faster though she was, gained on us only slowly. They held their fire for long minutes, while the little blob of light that was Craken's dome took shape in the forward microsonar screen.

Then they opened fire again—a full salvo this time, six missiles opening up like the ribs of a fan as they came toward us.

Roger twisted the *Dolphin's* tail, and we swung through violent evolutions.

Whump. Whumpwhump. Whumpwhumpwhump.

But they were all short, all exploding astern. Roger grinned crazily. "Maybe we'll make it! If we can hold out another ten minutes——"

"Missiles!" I cried, interrupting him. Another spreading salvo of bright little flecks leaped out from the pursuing shape in the microsonar screen.

Violent evasive action again ... and once again they all exploded astern.

But closer this time, much closer.

They were using up their missiles at a prodigious rate. Evidently Joe Trencher wanted to keep us from getting to that dome, at any cost!

The speaker from the engine room rattled and Bob's voice cried: "Bridge! We're going to have to cut power in three minutes! The reactor stops are all out. Repeat, we're going to have to cut power in three minutes!"

"Keep her going as long as you can!" Roger yelled. He slammed the conn wheel hard over, diving us sharply once more. "All hands!" he yelled. "All hands into pressure suits! The next salvo is likely to zero in right on our heads. We're bound to have hull leaks." He shook his head and grinned. "They'll fill us with water, but I'll get us in, wet or dry!"

In that moment, I had to admire Roger Fairfane. He wasn't the kind you could like very well—but the Academy doesn't make many mistakes, and I should have known that if he was a cadet at all, he was bound to have the stuff somewhere.

He caught me looking at him and he must have read the expression on my face, for he grinned. Even in the rush of that moment of wild flight he said: "You never liked me, did you? I don't blame you, Jim. There hasn't been much to like! I——" He licked his lips. "I have to admit something, Jim."

I said gruffly, "You don't have to admit anything——"

"No, no. I do." He kept his eyes on the microsonar, his hands on the conn wheel. He said quickly: "My father isn't a big shot, Jim! He's an accountant for Trident Lines, that's all. They let me use the boathouse at the Atlantic Manager's estate because they were sorry for

him. But I've always dreamed that some day, somehow——"

He broke off. Then he said somberly: "If I can help
open up another important route for Trident, down here
to the Tonga Trench, it'll be a big thing for my father!"

I shook my head silently. It was a funny thing. All
these months Bob and I had made fun of Roger, had
disliked him—and yet, underneath it all he was a fine,
likeable youth!

We all struggled into our pressure suits, keeping the
helmets cracked so we could maneuver better. Time
enough to seal up when the crashing missiles split our
hull open. . . .

And that time was almost at hand.

But first—the blare of a warning horn screamed at us.
Red warning lights blazed all over the instrument panel at
once, it seemed. The ceiling lights flickered and yellowed
as the current from the main engines flipped off and the
batteries cut in. The hurtling *Dolphin* faltered in her mad
rush through the sea.

The yell from the engine room told us what we already
knew: "Reactor out! We've lost our power. Batteries only
now!"

Roger looked at me and gave me a half-grin. There was
no bluster about him now, no pretense. He checked the
instrument panel and made his decision quickly.

He kicked the restraining stops on the conn wheel free,
and wrenched it up—far past normal diving angle, to the
absolute maximum it would travel. He stood the old
Dolphin right on her nose, heading straight down into the
abyss below.

Minutes passed. We heard the distant *whump* of missiles—but far above us now. Even with only battery
power to turn the screws, the *Dolphin* was dropping faster
than the missiles could travel, for gravity was pulling at us.

Roger kept his eyes glued to the microsonar and the
fathometers. At the last possible moment he pulled back
on the conn wheel; the diving vanes brought the ship into
a full-G pullout.

He cut the power to the screws.

In a moment there was a slithering, scraping sound from the hull, then a hard thud.

We had come to rest—without arms, without power, with twenty thousand feet of sea water over our heads, at the bottom in the Tonga Trench.

15

Abandon Ship!

We lay on the steep slope of the Tonga Trench, nearly four miles down, waiting for the *Killer* to finish us off.

Gideon and Bob Eskow came tumbling in from the engine room. "She's going to blow!" Bob yelled. "We ran the engines too long—the reactor's too hot. We've got to get out of here, Roger!"

Roger Fairfane nodded quietly, remotely. His face was abstracted, as though he were thinking out a classroom problem in sea tactics or navigation.

The microsonar was still working, after a fashion—one more drain on our batteries. I could see the blurred and dimmed image of the *Killer* on the topside screen. They were cricling far above us. Waiting.

The dead *Dolphin* lay onimously still, except for a faint pulsing from the circulator-tubes of the reactors. Nuclear reactions make no sound; there was nothing to warn us that an explosion was building a few yards away. Now and then there was an onimous creak of metal, an occasional snap, as though the underpowered edenite armor were yielding, millimeter by millimeter, to the crushing weight of the water above.

We lay sloping sharply, stern down. Roger stood with one hand on the conn-wheel to brace himself, staring into space.

He roused himself—I suppose it was only a matter of seconds—and looked around at us.

"Abandon ship!" he ordered.

And that was the end of the *Dolphin*.

We clustered in the emergency pressure-lock for a final council of war. Roger said commandingly: "We're only a few miles from Jason Craken's sea-mount. David, you lead the way. We'll have to conserve power, so only one of us will use his suit floodlamps at a time. Stay together! If anyone lags behind, he's lost. There won't be any chance of rescue. And we'll have to move right along. The air in the suits may not last for more than half an hour. The suit batteries are old; they have a lot of pressure to fight off. They may not last even as long as the air. Understand?"

We all nodded, looking around at each other.

We checked our depth armor, each inspecting the others'. The suits were fragile-seeming things, of aluminum and plastic. Only the glowing edenite film would keep them from collapsing instantly—and as Roger said, there wasn't much power to keep the edenite glowing.

"Seal helmets!" Roger ordered.

As we closed the faceplates, the edenite film on each suit of armor sprang into life, rippling faintly as we moved.

Roger waved an arm. Laddy Angel, nearest the lock valves, gestured his understanding of the order, and sprang to the locks.

The hatch behind us closed and locked.

The intake ports irised open and spewed fiercely driven jets of deep-sea water against the baffles.

Even the ricocheting spray nearly knocked us off our feet, but in a moment the lock was filled.

The outer hatch opened.

And we stepped out into the ancient sludge of the Tonga Trench, under four miles of water.

Behind us the hull of the *Dolphin* coruscated brightly. It seemed to light up the whole sea-bottom around us. I glanced back once. Shadows were chasing themselves over the edenite film—sure sign that the power was failing, that it was only a matter of time.

And then I had to look ahead.

We formed in line and started off, following David Craken. It took us each a few moments of trial-and-error to adjust our suits for a pound or two of weight— carefully balancing weight against buoyancy be valving off air—so that we could soar over the sludgy sea bottom in great, floating, slow-motion leaps.

And then we really began to cover ground.

In a moment the *Dolphin* behind us was a vague blur of bluish color. In another moment, it was only a faint, distant glow.

Yet—still there was light!

I cried: "What in the world!"—forgetting, for the moment, that no one could hear. It was incredible! Light—four miles down!

And more incredible still, there were things growing there.

The bottom of the sea is bare, black muck—nearly every square foot of it. Yet here there was vegetation. A shining forest of waving sea-fronds, growing strangely out of the rocky slope before us. Their thin, pliant stems rose upward, out of sight, snaking up into the shadows above. They carried thick, odd-shaped leaves——

And the leaves and trunks, the branches and curious flowers—every part of them glowed with soft green light!

I bounded ahead and tapped David Craken on the shoulder. The edenite films on my gauntlet and his shoulderpiece flared brightly as they touched; he could not have felt my hand, but must have seen the glow out of the corner of his eye. He turned stiffly, his whole body swinging around. I could see, dimly and murkily, his face behind the edenite-filmed plastic visor.

I waved my arm wordlessly at the glowing forest.

He nodded, and his lips shaped words—but I couldn't make them out.

Yet one thing came across—this was no surprise to him.

And then I remembered something: The strange watercolor Laddy Angel had showed me, hanging over David's bed at the Academy. It had portrayed a forest like this one, a rocky slope like this one—

And it had also shown something else, I remembered.

A saurian, huge and hideous, plunging through the submarine forest.

I had written off the submarine forest as a crazy fantasy—yet here it sprawled before my eyes. And the saurians?

I turned my mind to safer grounds—there was plenty of trouble right in front of us, without looking for more to worry about!

David seemed at home. We leaped lazily through the underwater glades in file, like monstrous slow-motion kangaroos on the Moon. After a few minutes, David signaled a halt. Gideon came up from his second place in the file to join David; Gideon's suit-lamps went on and Roger, who had led the procession with David, switched off his lights and fell back. It was a necessary precaution; the suit-lamps were blindingly bright—and terribly expensive of our hoarded battery power. We had to equalize the drain on our batteries—else one of us, with less reserve than the others, would sooner or later hear a warning creak of his flimsy suit armor as the edenite film flickered and faltered——

And that would be the last sound he heard on earth.

On and on.

Perhaps it had been only a few miles—but it seemed endless.

I began to feel queerly elated, faintly dizzy——

It took a moment for me to realize the cause: The old oxygen tanks were running low. We had not dared use power for electrolungs; the little tanks were for emergency use only.

Whatever the reason, I was breathing bad air.

Something shoved against my back, sent me sprawling. I heard a distant giant roar, rumbling through the water, and looked around to see that all of us had been tumbled about like straw men.

Gideon picked himself up and waved back toward the *Dolphin*. At once I understood.

The *Dolphin's* overwrought reactors had finally let go. Back behind us, a nuclear explosion had ripped the dead ship's hulk into atoms.

Thank heaven we were across the last ridge and out of range!

We picked ourselves up and moved on.

We were skirting the edge of an old lava flow, where molten stone from a sub-sea volcano had frozen into black, grotesque shapes. The weirdly gleaming sea-plants were all about us, growing out of the bare rock itself, it seemed.

I glanced at them—then again.

For a moment it seemed I had seen something moving in there. Something huge. . . .

It was impossible to tell. The only light was from the plants themselves, and it concealed as much as it showed. I paused to look again and saw nothing; and then I had to speed up to catch up with the others.

It was getting harder to put out a burst of extra speed.

There was no doubt about it now, the air in the suit was growing worse.

Down a long slope, and out over a plain. The glowing sea-plants still clustered thickly about us, everywhere. Above us the strange weeds made a ragged curtain between the black cliffs we had just passed.

David halted and waved ahead with a great spread-armed gesture.

I coughed, choked and tried to move forward. Then I realized that he was not calling for me to move up to the front of the column; Laddy Angel was already there.

David was showing us something.

I lifted my head to look. And there, peeping through the gaps in the sea-plants ahead, I could see the looming bulk of something enormous and black. A sea-mount! And atop it, like the gold on the Academy dome, a pale, blue glow shining.

Edenite! The glow was the dome of Jason Craken!

But I wondered if it were in time.

Someone—I couldn't tell who—stumbled and fell, struggled to get up, finally stood wavering, even buoyed up by the water. Someone else—Gideon, I thought—leaped to his side and steadied him with an arm.

Evidently it was not only my air which was going bad.

We moved ahead once more—but slower now, and keeping closer together.

Out of the corner of my eye I saw that flicker of movement again.

I looked, expecting to see nothing——

I was terribly, terribly wrong!

What I saw was far from nothing. It had been a faint, furtive glimpse of something huge and menacing.

And when I looked at it straight on, it was still there—huger, more menacing, real and tangible!

It was a saurian, giant and strange, and it was pacing us.

I turned on my suit-lamps, flooded the others with light to attract their attention. I waved frantically toward the monster in the undersea jungle.

And they saw. I could tell from the queer, contorted attitudes in which they stood that they saw.

David Craken made a wild, excited gesture, but I couldn't understand what he meant. The others, with one accord, leaped forward and scattered. And I was with them—all of us running, leaping, scurrying away in the slow, slow jumps the resistance of the water allowed. We dodged in among the tall, gently wavering stems of the sea-plants, looking for a hiding place.

I could hear my breath rasping inside the helmet, and the world was growing queerly black. There was a pounding in my head and a dull ache; the air was worse now, so bad that I was tempted to stop, to relax, to fall to the ground and rest, sleep, relax. . . .

I forced myself to squirm into the shelter of a clump of brightly glowing bushes. I lay on my back there, breathing raggedly and hard, and noticed without worry, without emotion, that the huge, strange beast was close upon me. Queer, I thought, it is just like David's painting—even to the rider on its back.

There *was* something on its back—no, not something, but someone. A person. A—a girl figure, slight and frail, brown-skinned, black-haired, her eyes glowing white as Joe Trencher's, her blue swim-suit woven of something as luminous as the weed. She was close, so close that I could see her wide-flaring nostrils, see the expression on her face.

It was easy enough to see, for she wore no pressure suit! Here four miles down, she was breathing the water of the Deeps!

But I had no time to study her, for the monster she rode took all my attention. Even in the poisoned calm of my slow suffocation, I knew that here was deadly danger. The enormous head was swaying down toward me, the great supple neck curving like a swan's. Its open mouth could have swallowed me in a single bite; its teeth seemed long as cavalry sabers.

The blue-gleaming forest turned gray-black and whirled about me.

I could see the detail of overlapping scales on the armored neck of the saurian, the enormous black claws that tipped its great oarlike limbs.

The gigantic head came down through the torn strands of shining weed, and I thought I had come to my last port. . . .

The grayness turned black. The blackness spun and roared around me.

I was unconscious, passed out cold.

16

Hermit of the Tonga Trench

I woke up with the memory of a fantastic dream— huge, hideous lizard things, swimming through the sea, with strange mermaids riding their backs and directing them with goads.

Fantastic! But even more fantastic was that I woke up at all!

I was lying on my back on a canvas cot, in a little metal-walled room. Someone had opened the helmet of my pressure suit, and fresh air was in my lungs!

I struggled up and looked about me.

Roger Fairfane lay on one side of me, Bob Eskow on the other. Both were still unconscious.

There was a pressure port in the wall of the room, and through it I could see a lock, filled with water under pressure. I could see something moving inside the lock— something that looked familiar, but strange at the same time.

It was both strange and familiar! The strange sea-girl, she was there! She had been no dream of oxygen starvation, but real flesh and blood, for now I saw her, pearl-eyed like the strange man named Joe Trencher . . . but with human worry and warm compassion on her face as she struggled to carry pressure-suited figures into the lock.

One—two—three! There were three of them, weakly stirring.

It was—it had to be—Gideon, Laddy and David. She had saved us all.

And behind her loomed the hulk of something strange and deadly—but she showed no fear. It was the gaping triangular face of the saurian.

As I watched, she turned about with an eel-like wriggle and slapped the monster familiarly on its horny nose. Not a blow in anger—but a caress, almost, as a rider might pat the muzzle of a faithful horse.

It was true, what David had said: The saurians were domesticated. The sea-creatures he called amphibians truly rode them, truly used them as beasts of burden.

The sea-girl left the saurian and swam inside. I saw her at the glowing dials of a control panel.

The great doors swung shut, closing out the huge, inquisitive saurian face. I saw the doors glow suddenly with edenite film.

Pumps began to labor and chug.

Floodlights came on.

In a moment the girl was standing on the wet floor of the lock, trying to tug at the pressure-suited figures of my friends toward the inner gate.

Bob Eskow twisted and turned and cried out sharply: "Diatom! Diatom to radiolarian. The molluscans are——"

He opened his eyes and gazed at me. For a moment he hardly recognized me.

Then he smiled. "I—I thought we were goners, Jim. Are you sure we're here?"

I slapped his pressure-suited shoulder. "We're here. This young lady and her friend, the dinosaur—they brought us to Craken's dome!"

David was already standing, stripping off his pressure suit. He nodded gravely. "Thank Maeva." He nodded to the girl, standing wide-eyed and silent, watching us. "If Maeva hadn't come along—— But Maeva and I have always been friends."

The girl spoke. It was queer, hearing human speech from what I still couldn't help thinking of as a mermaid!

But her voice was soft and musical as she said: "Please, David. Don't waste time. My people know you are here." She glanced at the lock port anxiously, as though she was expecting it to burst open, with a horde of amphibians or flame-breathing saurians charging through. "As we brought you to the dome, Old Ironsides and I, I saw another saurian with a rider watching us. Let us go to your father——"

David said sharply: "She's right. Come on!"

We were all of us conscious again. David and Gideon had never really passed out from the lack of oxygen, but they had been so weak that it was nearly the same thing. Without Maeva to help them, and the saurian she called "Old Ironsides" to bear them on its broad, scaly back, they would have been as dead as the rest of us.

Strange girl! Her skin was smooth and brown, her short-cut hair black. The pearly eyes, which on Joe Trencher had seemed empty and grim, on her seemed cool and gentle; they gave her face an expression of sadness, of wistfulness.

I thought that she was beautiful.

She was smiling at David, even in the urgency of that moment. I saw her hands flashing through a series of complicated motions—and realized that she was urging him on, to hurry to his father, in some sign language of the Deep that was more natural to her than speech.

Roger caught David's shoulder roughly and hauled him aside. He hissed, so that Maeva couldn't hear: "There aren't any mermaids! What—what sort of monster is she?"

David said angrily: "Monster? She's as human as you! She is one of the amphibians—like Joe Trencher, but one we can trust to be on our side. Her ancestors were the Polynesian islanders my father found trapped under the sea."

"But—but she's a fish, Craken! She breathes water! It isn't human!"

David's face stiffened, and for a moment I thought there might be trouble. He was furious.

But he calmed himself. Struggling for control— evidently this sea-girl meant something to him!—he said: "Come on! Let's find my father!"

We raced through the dome, along slippery steel hills, past rooms that, in the glimpse we caught as we passed, seemed like ancient chambers from a Sultan's palace, costly and beautiful and—falling into decay.

Fantastic place! A sub-sea dome is a fearfully expensive thing to construct—expensive not only of money, but of time and materials and human lives. There were hundreds upon hundreds of them scattered across the floors of the sea, true—but very few were those which were owned by a single man.

And to build one, as David Craken's father had built this, in secrecy, with only the help of a few technicians sworn to silence and the manual labor of the amphibians and the saurians—it was incredible!

I counted five levels below the topmost bulge of the dome—five levels packed with living quarters and recreation areas, with shops and docks and storage space, with a monster nuclear reactor chuckling away as it made the power to run the dome and keep the sea's might harmlessly away. There were rooms, a dozen of them or more, that looked like laboratories. We crossed through one that was lined with enormous vats, filled with the macerated remains of stalks of the strange, glowing weed that grew in the Trench outside. It was glowing only fitfully, fading almost into extinction here in the atmosphere; and the musty reek that rose from those vats nearly strangled poor Maeva—who was having a bad enough time out of the water anyway—and made the rest of us quicken our steps.

"Dad's experiments," David said briefly. "He's been trying to find the secret of the weed. He's tried everything—macerated them, dissolved them in acids, treated them with solvents, burned them, centrifuged them. Some day——" He glanced around at the benches of glassware, the bubbling beakers that reeked of acid, the racks of test tubes and distilling apparatus.

"Some day things will be different," David finished in an altered tone. "But now we have no time for this. Come on!"

We came to the topmost chamber of all.
There was no sign of David's father.

David said worriedly: "Maeva, I can't understand it! Where can he be?"

The sea-girl said, in her voice which was soft and liquid and occasionally gasping for breath: "He isn't well, David. He—he is not of the sea. Perhaps he is asleep." She touched David gently with her hand—and I saw with a fresh shock that the fingers were ever so slightly webbed. "You must take him up to the surface, David," she said, panting. "Or else I think he will die."

"I have to find him first!" David said worriedly. He cast about him, staring. We were in a room—once, it seemed, a luxurious salon. It was walled with books, thousands of them, stacked in shelves to the ceiling—titles of science and philosophy mixed helter-skelter with blood-and-thunder tales of danger and excitement. There were long, high shelves of portfolios of art works—left by David's mother when she passed away, I supposed, for they were gray with dust.

The room was now cluttered with more of the same tangle of scientific equipment we had seen below, as though the man who owned the dome had no interest left in life but his scientific researches. There were unpacked crates of glassware and reagents, with labels that showed he had bought them in Marinia, consignment tags that were addressed to a hundred fictitious names, none to himself. There was a cobalt "bomb" encased in tons of lead. A new electric autoclave that he had found no space for below. A big hydraulic press that could create experimental pressures a hundred times higher than those in the Deep outside. Test tubes and hypodermic needles and half-emptied bottles that Craken had labeled in hieroglyphics of his own.

The windows were the strangest thing in the room. They were wide picture windows, draped and curtained tastefully.

And the view in them was—rolling landscapes!

Outside those windows, four miles down, one saw spruce trees and tall pines, green mountain meadows and grassy foothills, far-off peaks that were white with snow!

I stared at them incredulously. David glanced at me, then half-smiled. "Stereoscapes," he said carelessly, his eyes roaming about, his mind far away. "They were for my mother. She came from Colorado, and always she longed for the dry land and the mountains of her home. . . ."

Maeva's voice came imploringly: "David! We must hurry."

He said, worriedly, "I don't know what to do, Maeva! I suppose the best thing is for us to fan out and search the dome. But——"

We never heard the end of that sentence.

There was a sudden scratching sound that seemed to permeate the dome. Then a blare of noise, from dozens of concealed loudspeakers.

The mechanical voice of an electric watchman roared: "Attention! Attention! The dome is under attack! Attention, attention! The dome is under attack!"

Roger said in a panicky voice: "David, let's do something! Forget your father. The amphibians, they're attacking and——"

But David wasn't listening to him.

David was staring, across the room, toward a clutter of equipment and gear that nearly filled one corner.

"Dad!" he cried.

We all whirled.

There, in the corner, an old man, wasted and gaunt, was sitting up, propping himself on a cot. He had been out of sight behind the tangled junk that surrounded him.

The warning of the electronic watchman had waked him.

He was sitting up, calm as can be, his eyes remote but friendly, his expression unperturbed. He wore a little beard—once dapper, now scraggly and gray.

"Why, David," he said. "I've been wondering where you were. How nice that you've brought some friends to visit us."

17

Craken of the Sea-Mount

We looked at him, and then at each other. The same thought was in all our minds, I could see it in the eyes of David and the sea-girl, reflected on the faces of the others.

Jason Craken's mind was going.

He beamed at us pleasantly. "Welcome," he said. "Welcome to you all."

Once he had been a powerful man. I could see that, from the size of his bones and the lean muscles that he had left. But he was wasted now, and gaunt. His skin hung loose, and it was mottled with a queer greenish stain. His gray hair needed cutting, and the beard was a tangle. There was almost no trace left of the dandy my uncle had described.

He had been sleeping in his laboratory smock—once white, now wrinkled and stained. He glanced down at it and chuckled.

He said ruefully, "I was not expecting guests, as you can see. I do apologize to you. I dislike greeting my son's guests in so unkempt an array. But my experiments, gentlemen, my experiments take all too much of my time. One has not enough hours in the day for all the many ——"

David stepped over to him. He said gravely, "Father. Why don't you rest a bit? I'll show the—the guests around the dome."

And all this time the robot watchman was howling: *Attention, attention, attention!*

David signaled to us and we left the room quietly. In a moment he joined us. "He'll be all right," he said. "Now— let's go to the conn room!"

The conn room was a tiny chamber at the base of the dome, ringed by televisor screens, where a picture of the sea-floor all about the dome was in mosaic patches.

There was nothing in sight.

David nodded worriedly. "Not yet," he commented. "I thought not. The robot watchman—it is set to warn of approaching sub-sea vessels, but it has a considerable range. They won't be in sight for a while yet."

"They?" I demanded.

David shrugged. "I don't know if there will be more than one. The *Killer Whale,* perhaps—but the amphibians had another sea-car that I know of, the one they took from me. How many besides that I don't know."

Gideon said softly, his brow furrowed: "Bad luck, I think. I'd hoped that they would believe we had all gone up with the *Dolphin* when the reactor exploded."

The sea-girl shook her head. "I told you," she reminded him, gasping. "We were seen. I—I am sorry, David, that I let them see me, but——"

"Maeva! Don't apologize. You saved our lives!" David wrung her hand. He looked thoughtfully at the screens, then nodded.

"I've got to look after my father," he said. "Jim, will you come with me? The rest of you—it would be better if you stayed here, kept an eye on the screens."

Gideon nodded. "Fine," he agreed, in his gentle voice. "Then—that's a Mark XIX fire-control director I see there? And a turret gun, I suppose? Yes. Then we can fight them off, if need be, right from here. I've handled the Mark XIX before and——"

David interrupted him.

"I don't think you can do much with this one," he said.

Gideon looked at him thoughtfully. "And why not?" he asked after a moment.

David said: "It's broken, Gideon. The amphibians destroyed the circuits when they rebelled against my father. If they do attack—we have no weapons to fight them with."

We left them behind us, and I must say the heart was out of me. Nothing to fight with! Not even a sea-car to escape in, now!

But Gideon was already at work before we left the fire-control room, stripping down the circuit-junction mains, checking the ruined connections. It was very unlikely that he could repair the gun. But Gideon had done some very unlikely things before.

David's father was asleep again when we came back to him. David woke him gently.

He rubbed his eyes and blinked at David.

This time there was none of that absent serenity with which he had greeted us before. He seemed to remember what was going on about him—and he seemed to be in despair.

"David," he said. "David——"

He shook himself and stood up.

He stumbled weakly to a laboratory, filled a little glass beaker out of a bottle of colorless fluid and gulped it down.

He came back to us, smiling and walking more steadily.

"Sit down," he said, "sit down." He shoved piles of books off a couple of chairs. "I had given you up, David. It is good to see you."

David Craken hurried to find another chair for the old man, but he ignored it. He sat down on the edge of the creaking cot and ran his hands through his thinning hair.

David said: "Dad, you're sick!"

Jason Craken shrugged. "A few unfortunate reactions." He glanced absently at the strange green blotches on his hands. "I suppose I've been my own guinea pig a few times too many. But I'm strong enough, David. Strong enough—as Joe Trencher will find—to take back what belongs to me!"

His eyes were hollowed and bloodshot, yet strangely intense with a light that came from fever—or madness, I thought. He beckoned to us with his gnarled, lean hand.

David said: "Dad—we're being attacked! Didn't you know that? The robot warning came ten minutes ago."

Jason Craken shook his head impatiently. He made a careless gesture, as though he was brushing the attackers away. "There have been many attacks," he boomed, "but I am still here. And I will stay here while I live. And when I am gone—you shall stay after me, David."

He stood up, swaying slightly, and walked over to the laboratory bench once more for another beaker of the colorless fluid. Whatever it was, it seemed to put new life into him. He said strongly: "Joe Trencher will learn! I'll conquer him as we've conquered the saurians, David!" He came back and sat beside us, a scarecrow emperor with that rumpled cot for a throne. He turned to me. "Jim Eden," he said, "I welcome you to Tonga Trench. I never thought I would need the help your uncle promised, so many years ago. But I never thought that Trencher and his people would turn against me!"

He seemed to be both raging with fury and morbidly depressed. "Trencher!" he spat. "I assure you, Jim Eden, that without my help the amphibians would still be living the life of animals! That was how I found them—trapped in their own submerged caves. If I were an egotist, I could say that I created them, and it would be near to the truth. Yet—they are ungrateful! They have turned against me! They and the saurians, I must crush them, show them who is the master——"

He broke off suddenly as his voice reached a crescendo. For a moment he sat there, staring at us wildly.

David went to him, patted him and soothed him, calmed him down. It was hard to tell there, for a moment, which was the parent and which the child.

But one thing I knew.

David Craken's father was nearly mad!

Yet—he could talk as sanely as anyone in the world, between attacks of his raging obsession.

David quieted him down, and we sat there for what seemed a long time, talking, waiting. Waiting—I hardly hardly knew what we were waiting for.

Queer interlude! The robot watchman had been cut off, its mindless cries of warning no longer battered against our ears. Yet—we were still under attack! There had not yet been a jet missile fired against us, but the robot could not have made a mistake.

There was no doubt about it: Somewhere just outside the range of the microsonars, Joe Trencher and the *Killer Whale* swung, getting ready to batter down the dome we were in.

And we had no weapons.

I knew that Gideon would be racing against time, trying to fit the maimed circuits of the gun controls back into some semblance of order—but it was a long, complex job. It was something a trained crew might take a week to do—and he was one man, working on unfamiliar components!

But somehow, in that room with Jason Craken and his son, I was not afraid.

After a bit he collected himself again and began to talk of my father and my uncle. Astonishing how clearly he recollected every detail of those days, decades ago—and could hardly remember how he had lived in the months he had been alone here, while David and the rest of us were preparing to come to help him!

David whispered to me: "Talk to him about his experiments and discoveries. It—it helps to keep him steady."

I said obediently: "Tell me about—ah—tell me about those queer plants outside the dome. I've been under the sea before this, Mr. Craken, but I've never seen anything like them!"

He nodded—it was like an eagle nodding, the fierce face quiet, the eyes hooded. "No one else has either, Jim Eden! The deeps are a funnel—a funnel of life. Everywhere but here. Do you understand what I mean by that?"

I nodded eagerly—even there, with the danger of destruction hanging over us all, I couldn't help being held by that strange old man. "One of my instructors said that," I told him. "I remember. He said that life in the ocean is a funnel, filled from the top. Tiny plants grow near the surface, where the sunlight reaches them. They make food for tiny creatures that eat them—and the tiny animal creatures are eaten by larger ones, and so on. But everything depends on the little plants at the surface, making food for the whole sea out of sunlight. Only a few crumbs get down the spout of the funnel, to the depths."

"Quite true!" boomed the old man. "And here we have another funnel, Jim Eden. But one that is upside down. Those plants——" he looked at me sharply, almost suspiciously. "Those plants are the secret of the Tonga Trench, Jim Eden. It is the greatest secret of all, for on them depend all the other wonders of my kingdom of the Trench. They have their own source of energy! It is an atomic process." He frowned at me thoughtfully. "I—I have not finally succeeded in penetrating all of its secrets," he confessed. "Believe me, I have tried. But it is a nuclear reaction of some sort—deriving energy, I believe, from the unstable potassium isotope in sea water. But I have not yet been able to get the process to work in a test tube. Not yet. But I will!"

He got up and walked more slowly, thoughtfully, to the laboratory bench. Absently he poured himself another beaker of the elixir on which he seemed to be absolutely dependent. He looked at it thoughtfully and then set it down, untasted.

Evidently the thought of the secret of the Tonga Trench was as powerful a stimulant to him as the elixir! I began to see how this man had been able to keep going for so long, alone and sick—he was driven by the remorseless compulsion that makes great men . . . and maniacs.

"So you see," he said, "there is a second funnel of life here. The shining weed, with its own energy, that does not need the light of the sun. The little animals that feed off it. The larger ones—the saurians and the amphibians—that live off the small."

"The saurians," I broke in, strangely excited. "David said something about—about some sort of danger from them. Is it true?"

"Danger?" The old man stared at his son with a hint of reproof. As though the word had been a trigger that set him off, he picked up the beaker of fluid and swallowed it. "Danger? Ah, David—you cannot fear the saurians! They cannot harm us in the dome!" He turned to me, and once again assumed the tone and attitude of a schoolmaster, lecturing a pupil. "It is a matter of breeding patterns," he said soberly. "'The saurians are egg-layers, and their eggs cannot stand the pressures of the bottom of the Trench, where the shining weeds grow. So each year—at the time of the breeding season—they must come up to the top of the sea-mount, to lay their eggs. There is only one way to the caves where, from ages past, they had always laid them—and I built this dome squarely across it!"

He chuckled softly, as though he had done a clever thing. "While they were tamed," he told me gleefully, "I permitted them to pass. But now—now they shall not enter their caves! This Trench is mine, and I intend to keep it!"

He paused, staring at me.

"I may need help," he admitted at last. "There are many saurians—— But you are here! You and the others, you must help me. I can pay you. I can pay very well, for all the wealth of the Tonga Trench is mine. Tonga pearls! I have found a way to increase the yield—like the old Japanese cultured-pearl fishers, years ago. It cannot be done with ordinary oysters, for the Tonga pearls must have the radioactive nucleus that comes from the shining weed. But I have planted Tonga pearls, Jim Eden, and the first harvest is ready to be gathered!"

He stood up. Bent as he was, he towered over us.

"I offer you a share in a thousand thousand Tonga pearls for your help! You owe me that help anyway, as you know—for your father and your uncle have promised it. What do you say, Jim Eden? Will you help me hold the empire of the Tonga Trench?"

His eyes were growing wilder and wilder.

"Here is what you must do!" he cried. "You must take your subsea cruiser, the *Dolphin*. You must destroy the ship Joe Trencher is using. The dome's own armaments will suffice for the saurians—I have a most powerful missile gun mounted high on the dome, well supplied with ammunition, with the latest automatic fire-control built in. Crush Joe Trencher for me—the dome itself will destroy the saurians if they try to come through. Is that agreed, Jim Eden?"

And that was when the bubble burst.

He stood waiting for my answer. He had nearly made me believe that these things were possible, for a moment. He was so absolutely sure of himself, that I forgot, while he was speaking, a few things.

For instance——

The *Dolphin* was destroyed, blown to atoms.

His missile gun was not working, sabotaged by the amphibians when they turned against him.

David Craken and I stared at each other somberly, while the crazed light faded and died in his father's eyes.

For Jason Craken's mind was wandering again. He had fought the sea too long, and taken too much of his own strange potions.

He had conceived a battle scheme—a perfect tactical

plan, except that it relied on a gun that would not fire and a ship that had been sunk!

I don't know what we would have said to him then.

But it turned out that we didn't have to say anything.

There was a scratching, racing sound of foosteps from outside and the sea-girl, Maeva, burst gasping and frantic into the room.

"David!" she cried raggedly, fighting for breath. "David, they're coming back! The saurians are attacking again, and there is a subsea ship leading them!"

We leaped to our feet.

But even before we got out of the room, a dull explosion rocked the dome.

A sub-sea missile from the *Killer!* The fight for Tonga Trench had begun!

18

The Fight for Tonga Trench

"Up!" cried Maeva. "Up to the missile-gun turret. Gideon couldn't fix the fire-control equipment—he's trying to handle the gun manually!"

We pounded up narrow steel stairs, David flying ahead.

We found Gideon in the turret, his eyes on a complicated panel of wires and resistors, his mind so fixed on his task that he didn't even look up to see us come in.

"Gideon!" I cried—and then had to stop, holding onto the wall, as another explosion rocked the dome.

They meant business this time!

The turret was tiny and gloomy, and filled with the reek that rose from Jason Craken's laboratories below. There were tiny windows spotted about it—not much more than portholes, really—and there was little to see through them. All I could make out, through the pale glimmer of the edenite film on the window itself, was the steep curve of the dome beneath us, glowing unsteadily with its own film. The cold blue light from the dome caught two or three jutting points of dark rock.

Beyond that, the darkness of the deep was broken only by the occasional ghostly glimmerings of deep-sea creatures that carried lights of their own.

I glanced at David, startled. "I don't see anything!"

He nodded. "You wouldn't, Jim. You need microsonar to see very far under the surface of the sea. That's what Gideon is working on now, I should judge. This missile gun—it can be worked manually, if its microsonar sights are working. But it's been fifteen years at least since it was manned—always it was controlled from the fire-control chamber below, you see. And that is wrecked. . . ."

Gideon glanced up abstractedly. He nodded agreement, started to speak, and returned to his work.

It wasn't hard to see that he was worried.

The missile gun almost filled the turret. It was an ugly, efficient machine of destruction, though the firing tube, what little of it was within its turret, looked oddly slim. The bright-cased missiles racked in the magazine weren't much larger than my arm.

"Looks old-fashioned to you?" David was reading my mind. "But it's deadly enough, Jim. One of those shells will destroy a sea-car—the shock neutralizes the edenite film for a tiny fraction of a second. And the sea's own pressure does the rest. They're steam jets—athodyds, they're called; they scoop up water and fire it out behind in the form of steam."

There was a sudden exclamation from Gideon.

He plucked something out of a kit of spare parts, plugged a new component into the tangle of wires and sub-assemblies.

"That should do it!" he said softly. And he touched a switch.

We all stood waiting, almost holding our breaths.

There was a distant hum of tiny motors.

The turret shuddered and turned slightly.

The microsonar screen came to life.

"You've done it!" David cried.

Gideon nodded. "It works, at any rate." He patted the slim breech, almost fondly. "Anyway, I think it does. It was the sonar hookup that was the big headache. It serves as the sights for the missile-gun. Without the sonar, it would be like firing blind. Now—I think we can see what we're doing."

I stared into the microsonar, fascinated. It was an old, old model—hardly like the bright new screen the Academy had taught me to work with. Everything was reduced and distorted, as though we were looking into the wrong end of a cheap telescope.

But, as I grew used to it, I could pick some details out. I could see the steep slopes of the sea-mount falling away from us. I found the jagged rim of a ravine—the one the saurians used for their breeding trail, no doubt; the same one that Maeva and Old Ironsides had carried us along.

I glanced at the screen, and then again.

There was a whirling pattern of tiny shapes. For a moment I couldn't make them out. Then I said: "Why, it's a school of fish. At least that proves the saurians aren't around, doesn't it? I mean, they would frighten the fish away and——"

"Fish?" Gideon was staring at me. "What are you talking about?"

I said patiently, "Why, Gideon, don't you see? If there were saurians, they'd show in the microsonar, wouldn't they? And that school of fish——"

He looked at me with a puzzled expression, then shrugged.

"Jim," he said, "look here." He adjusted the verniers of the microsonar with a delicate touch, bringing into sharp focus. He pointed. "There," he said. "Right in front of you. Saurians—a couple of hundred of them, I'd guess. They look pretty small, because these old target screens reduce everything—but there they are, just out of range!"

I stared, unbelieving.

What he was pointing at was what I had thought was a school of tiny fish!

They were saurians, all right—hundreds upon hundreds of them. I looked more closely, and I could see another little object among my "fish"—not a saurian this time, but something infinitely more dangerous.

I pointed to it. Gideon and David followed my pointing finger.

"That's right, Jim," said David. "It's the *Killer Whale*. They're waiting. . . . But they won't wait much longer."

They waited exactly five more minutes.

Then all three of us saw the little spurt of light jet out from the *Killer's* bright outline and come arrowing in toward us. Another jet missile!

Seconds later, the dull boom of its explosion shook the dome once more.

But even before that, Gideon had leaped into the cradle of the missile-gun. One hand on the trips, the other coaxing the best possible image from the microsonar sights, he wheeled the turret to bring the weapon to bear on the distant shape of the *Killer Whale.* I saw him press the trips——

There was a staccato rapping, and the slim breech of the missile-gun leaped a fraction of an inch, half a dozen times, as Gideon fired a salvo of six missiles at the *Killer.*

The microsonar flared six times as the missiles went off, in a blast of pressure waves.

When the screen cleared—the *Killer Whale* still hung there, surrounded by its cluster of circling saurians.

Gideon nodded soberly. "Out of range, of course. But we're at extreme range too. Even with the better weapons they have on the cruiser. At least we can hope to keep them at arm's length." He checked the loading bays of the missile-gun. "Jim, David," he said. "Reload for me, will you? I don't want to get away from the trigger, in case Trencher and his boys decide to make a sudden jump."

We leaped to do as he asked. The stacks of missiles in their neat racks around the turret were none too many for our needs. We filled the bays—the gun's own automatic loading mechanism would take over from there—and looked worriedly at the dwindling pile of missiles that were left.

"Not too many," David conceded. "Gideon, will you be all right here alone? Jim and I had best go down to the storeroom for more missiles."

"I'll be all right!" Gideon's smile flashed white. "But don't take too long. I have a feeling we're going to need every missile we can get any minute now!"

But the attack didn't come.

We rounded up a work party, David and I. Bob and Laddy and Roger Fairfane formed teams to haul clips of the slim missiles from the storerooms at the base of the dome, up to the missile turret. Three of them was a load for one man; we made two or three trips apiece.

And still the attack didn't come.

And then David and Bob came out of the storeroom with only one missile apiece. David's face was ghastly white.

"They're gone!" he said tensely. "This is all that is left. The amphibians—when they turned against my father, they cleaned out the armory too, all but a few missiles we've found."

We made a quick count. About seventy-five rounds, no more.

And the missile gun fired in bursts of half a dozen!

We held a quick council of war in the conn room at the base of the dome, near the storage chambers. The screens that ringed it showed a mosaic of the sea-mount and sea-bottom around us.

The *Killer Whale* still hung there, still threatening, still waiting. At odd intervals they loosed a missile, but none of them had caused any damage; we had come to ignore them. And the saurians still milled about in their racing schools.

David said somberly: "It's the beginning of their breeding season. I suppose for millions of years they've been doing it just that way. They go through that strange sort of ritual, down there at the base of the sea-mount, working themselves up. I've seen it many times. They go on like that for hours. And then at last, one of them will start up the side of the sea-mount, toward the caves, where they will lay their eggs. And then all the others will follow——"

He closed his eyes. I could imagine what he was seeing in his mind's eye: A horde of saurians, hundreds strong, streaming up the side of the sea-mount, battering past the dome. And with Joe Trencher in his *Killer Whale* riding herd on them, driving them against the dome itself, while he pounded it with missiles!

The edenite dome—yes, it was strong, no doubt! But each of those beasts was nearly the size of a whale. Twenty or thirty tons of fiercely driven flesh pounding against the dome would, at the least, shake it. Multiply that by a hundred, two hundred, three hundred—and remember that the edenite film was after all maintained only by the power that came from delicate electronic parts. If for one split fraction of a second the power faltered. . . .

Then in moments the dome would be flat.

And we would be crushed blobs of matter in a tangle of wreckage, as four miles of sea stamped us into the muck.

Bob Eskow mopped his brow and stood up.

He turned to David Craken.

"David," he said, "that settles it. The missile-gun might stop the saurians—but with only seventy-five rounds for it, and hundreds of the saurians, we might as well not bother. And we'll never get the *Killer Whale* with the gun; it isn't powerful enough, hasn't got the range. There's only one thing to do."

I said: "He's right, David. It's up to you. You've got to make peace with the amphibians."

David looked at us strangely.

"Make peace with them!" He laughed sharply. "If I only could! But, don't you see? My father—he is the one who must make peace. And his mind is—is wandering. You've seen it for yourselves. The amphibians aren't used to the world, you know. They understand the rule of one man, a leader. Joe Trencher is their leader; and Joe once bowed to the rule of my father. I don't say my father was always right. He was a stern man. Perhaps all along, his mind was a little—well, strained. He's been through enough to strain anyone! But he was perhaps a little too severe, a little too unyielding. And so Joe Trencher's people turned against him.

"But it is my father they still respect, even though they are fighting him. If he would try to make peace—yes, that might work. But he never will. He can't. His mind simply cannot accept it."

I said, suddenly struck by a thought: "David! This must have happened before, hasn't it? I don't mean the rebellion of the amphibians, but the breeding season of the saurians. What did you do other years, when they made their procession up to the caves in the sea mount? How did you keep them from damaging the dome?"

David shrugged wretchedly. "The amphibians herded

them," he said. "We would station a dozen of them outside the dome with floodlights and gongs. Sound carries under water, you know—and the sound of the gongs and the light from the floods would keep them away from the dome. Oh, we had a good many narrow escapes—my father never should have built his dome right here, in their track. But he is a willful man.

"But without the amphibians to help us—with them attacking at the same time—it's hopeless."

There was no more time for discussion.

We heard a dull crunch of another jet missile from the *Killer Whale*—and then another, and a third, almost at once.

And simultaneously, the light, staccato rattle of our own turret missile-gun, as Gideon, high above us, fired in return.

We all turned to stare at the mosiac of the sea-mount below us.

The herd of saurians were milling purposelessly no longer. Two, three, four of them had started coming up toward us—more were following.

And the glittering hull of the *Killer Whale* was coming in with them, firing as it came.

19

Sub-Sea Stampede!

The dome was thundering and quivering under the almost incessant fire from the *Killer Whale*.

Gideon was returning their fire—coolly, desperately ... and in the end, hopelessly. But he was managing to keep the saurians in a state of confusion. He had beaten back the first surge of a handful of the enormous beasts. The main herd had milled a bit more, than another batch had made the dash for their breeding trail past the dome. The explosions of our little missile-gun had demoralized and confused them.

There had been a third attempt, and a fourth.

And each time Gideon had managed to rout the monsters. But I had kept a rough count, and I knew what Gideon knew: We were nearly out of missiles.

I thought of Gideon, clinging desperately to his missile-gun high above, and felt regret. This wasn't his fight; I had got myself into it, but I blamed myself for involving Gideon.

But I didn't have much time for such thoughts, for we were busy.

David had had one desperate idea: We would recharge the little oxygen flasks in our pressure suits, feed as much charge into the batteries as they would take, and try at the last to go out into the deep with the lights and the gongs, to see if we could herd the saurians away from the dome.

The idea was desperation itself—for surely the amphibians, stronger and better-equipped, would be driving the frantic monsters in upon us, and there was little doubt that it was going to be a harrowingly unsafe place to be, out at the base of the dome, under four miles of water, with thirty-ton saurians milling and raving about in frenzy.

But it was the only chance we had.

Jason Craken was mooning about by himself, talking excitedly in gibberish; Gideon and Roger were fully occupied in the turret. It left only Laddy, David, the sea-girl Maeva, and myself to try to get the suits ready for us.

For Bob Eskow was nowhere to be seen.

It took us interminable minutes, while the dome rocked and quivered under our feet. Then David threw down the last oxygen cylinder angrily. "No more gas in the tank!" he cried. "We'll have to make do with what we have. How do we stand, Laddy?"

Laddy Angel, fitting cylinders into the suits, counted rapidly and shrugged.

"It is not good, my friend David," he said softly. "There is not much oxygen——"

"I know that! How much?"

Laddy frowned and squinted thoughtfully. "Perhaps—perhaps twenty minutes for each suit. Four suits. We have enough oxygen for four of us to put on suits and go out into the abyss, to try to frighten away your saurians. Only——" he shrugged. "It is what they teach at the Academy," he confessed, "but I am not sure it is true here. So many cubic centimeters of oxygen, so many seconds of safe breathing time. But I cannot be sure, David, if the instructors in my classroom were thinking of such a use of breath as we shall be making! We must leap and pound gongs and jump about like cheerleaders at a football game, and I have some doubt that the air that would last twenty minutes of quiet walking about will last as long while we cavort like acrobats."

David demanded feverishly: "Power?"

That was my department. I had hooked the leyden-type batteries onto the dome's own power reactor, watched the gauges that recorded the time.

"Not much power," I admitted. "But if we only have twenty minutes of breathing time, it doesn't matter. The power will hold the edenite armor on the suits for at least twice that."

David stood thoughtfully silent for a moment.

Then he shrugged. "Well," he said, "it's the best we can do. If it isn't good enough——"

He didn't finish the sentence.

He didn't have to, because we all knew what it meant if we failed.

Lacking oxygen and power, we could be out on the floor of the sea for only a few minutes—so we had to wait there in the conn room until the stampede was raging upon us. We watched the mosaic screens for the sign of the big rush, the rush that Gideon with his missile-gun would not be able to stem.

We didn't speak much; there wasn't much left to say.

And I remembered again: Bob Eskow was missing.

Where had he got to? I said: "David—Bob's been gone a long time. We'll need him—when we go outside."

David frowned, his eyes intent on the screen. "He was rummaging through the storerooms—looking for more oxygen cylinders, I think, though I told him there weren't any. Perhaps one of us should look for him." He turned to the sea-girl, Maeva, who stood silently by, watching us with wide, calm eyes. I envied her! If the saurians blundered through our weak defenses and the dome came pounding down—she at least would live!

And then I remembered Joe Trencher and his blazing

anger against everything connected with the Crakens, and I wasn't so sure that she would live, after all. For surely Joe Trencher would not spare a traitor to the amphibian people, one who took the side of the Crakens against them.

"Maeva," he told her, "see if you can find him."

She nodded, gasping for breath, and started soundlessly out of the conn room. But she didn't have to go far, for as she reached the door Bob appeared on the other side.

We all stared at him. He was lugging a huge, yellow-painted metal cylinder, a foot thick and as long as Bob himself. Black letters were stenciled on the yellow:

DEEP SEA SURVIVAL KIT
Contents: Four-place raft, with emergency survival and signal equipment. Edenite shield tested to twenty thousand feet.

"What in the world are you going to do with that?" I demanded.

He looked up, startled, and out of breath. "We can reach radiolarian, don't you see? I mean——"

"*What?*"

He broke off, and some of the absorbed gleam faded from his eyes. "I mean——" he hesitated. "I mean, if a couple of us took it to the surface, we could, well, summon the Fleet. We would be able to——"

He went on, while I stared at him. Bob was acting very queerly, I thought. Could he be going to pieces under the strain of our situation? I was sure he had said something about "radiolarian"—the same sort of jumbled nonsense he was muttering when he woke up after Maeva had rescued us.

But he *seemed* perfectly all right. . . .

David told him sharply: "Wait, Bob. It's a pretty idea, but there are two things wrong with it. In the first place, we're pretty far off the beaten track here—and you have no guarantee that there would be a Fleet vessel anywhere around to receive your message." Bob opened his mouth to say something; David stopped him. "And even more important—we don't have that much time. One of those survival kit buoys will haul you up to the surface easily enough, I admit. But it takes at least ten minutes from this far down—even assuming you can hold on while you're being jerked up at twenty or thirty miles an hour!" He glanced at the microsonar screens worriedly. "We may not even have ten minutes!"

We didn't.

In fact, we didn't have ten seconds.

There was a rattle from the intercom that connected with the missile-gun turret high above, and Gideon's soft voice came to us crying: "Stand by for trouble! They're coming fast!"

We didn't need that warning. In our own microsonar screens we could see the saurians streaming toward us— not just two or three this time, but a solid group of a score or more, and the whole monstrous herd following close behind!

We crowded into the lock, the four of us in pressure suits and the sea-girl, Maeva, close beside.

The sea came in around us.

Under that tremendous pressure, it didn't flow in a stream from the valve. It exploded into a thundering fog that blinded our face plates and tore at our suits like a wild white hurricane.

The thunder stopped at last. We stepped out onto the slope of the sea-mount to face the greater thunder from the rampaging saurians.

Endless minutes! We spread out, the five of us, with suit-lamps and gongs and tiny old explosive grenades David had dug up from somewhere—too small to do much harm, big enough to make a startling noise.

The saurians came down on us in hordes. It seemed like thousands of them, clustered as thick as bees on a field of August clover. It was impossible to believe that we five, with the pathetic substitutes for arms we carried, could do anything to divert that tide of Juggernauts.

But we tried.

We flashed our lights at them, and tossed our grenades. We beat the huge brass gongs David had given us, and the low mellow booming sound echoed and multiplied in the terrible pressure of the Trench.

We terrified the monsters.

I think that they would have fled from the field entirely—if it had been only them.

But as we were driving them from one side, so were others from behind. The amphibians! A dozen or more of the saurians carried low-crouched riders, jabbing at them with long, pointed goads, driving them in upon us. And other amphibians swam behind the maddened herd, making nearly as much noise as we, causing nearly as much panic in the beasts.

It seemed to go on forever. . . .

And I began to feel faint and weak. The air was giving out!

I looked about feverishly, fighting to stay conscious. I could see Maeva and David Craken to one side, doggedly leaping and pounding their gongs like mad undersea puppets. Farther down the slope, toward the fringe of shining weed that stopped short of the dome, I saw Laddy Angel dodging the onslaught of a pair of great saurians, leaping up after them and driving them away from the dome. It was hard to see, in the pale blue glow that shone from Jason Craken's edenite fortress, but—where was Bob?

Look as I might, I couldn't see him anywhere.

I reeled and nearly fell, even buoyed up by the water.

I must have used up my oxygen even sooner than we had figured. I choked and blinked and tried to focus on the round, blue-lit bulk of the dome—so far away!

I took a step toward it—and another——

It seemed impossibly far away.

20

"The Molluscans Are Ripe!"

Yards short of the dome I toppled and slowly fell, and I had not the strength to stand up again—little though I needed with the buoying water to help.

Everything was queerly blurred, strangely unimportant. I knew my air was bad. I could live a few more minutes—perhaps even a quarter of an hour—but I couldn't move, for there simply was not air enough left in my tanks to sustain me.

It was perfectly obvious. I would lie there, I thought drowsily, lazily, until I fell asleep. And then, after some minutes, I would die, poisoned by the carbon dioxide from my own breath. . . .

Or perhaps, if the edenite shield faltered first as the power ran out, crushed into a shapeless mass by the fury of the deeps.

It was perfectly obvious, and I couldn't bring myself to care.

Something strange was happening. I raised my head slightly to see better. There was a queer, narrow metal cave, and something moving around in it—something with a bright yellow head and a bright yellow body——

I shook my head violently to clear it and looked again.

The cave became the airlock of the dome.

The queer object with the bright yellow head became Bob Eskow, wearing his pressure suit and carrying—carrying that yellow cylinder he had lugged up from the storerooms, the emergency escape kit.

I thought in a dreamy way how remarkable it was that he should be bothering with something like that. But I didn't really care. All I felt was an overwhelming laziness—narcosis, from bad air rather than pressure, but narcosis all the same. It didn't matter. Nothing mattered.

Suddenly Bob was tugging at me.

That didn't matter either, but he was interfering with my pleasant lazy rest. I pushed at him angrily. I couldn't make out what he was doing.

Then I saw: He was binding me to the shackles around the yellow-painted rescue buoy. For a moment his helmeted face hung in front of mine, huge and dim. I saw him gesture vehemently with a chopping motion.

I stared at him, irritated and puzzled. Chop? What did he mean?

I glanced behind me, and saw the end of the yellow rescue buoy, where the deadweight was shackled to the flotation unit. The idea was to uncouple the weight and drop it off, then the buoy would surge toward the surface, carrying its rescued passengers with it.

Possibly that was what Bob wanted me to do—knock the weights loose.

Fretfully I pressed the release lever. The weighted end of the cylinder sprang free.

And the flotation unit jerked us toward the surface.

It was fast! It was almost like being fired from a cannon. The shock made me black out for a second, I think. I was conscious of the black rock and the shimmering blue dome falling away beneath us, and then things became very confused. There was a fading gray glow in the water about us, then only darkness. Then I began to see queer bright lights—shining eyes, they seemed, that dived at us from above and dropped rapidly away beneath.

The air was growing rapidly worse.

I could hear myself breathing—great, rapid, panting upheavals, like Maeva after hours of breathing air, like a dying man. I began to have a burning in my lungs. My head ached . . . great gongs beat and spirals of fire spun and vanished in the dark sea.

And then suddenly, we were at the surface of the sea.

Amazingly, it was night!

Somehow I had not thought of its being night-time above. We cracked our faceplates, clinging to the buoy, and I breathed deeply of cool, damp, night air. I stared at the stars as though I had never seen a night sky before. Amazing!

But what was most amazing was that we were alive.

As the air hit me it was like a dose of the strongest stimulant known to man. I coughed and choked and, if I hadn't been bound to the buoy, I think I might have dropped free and sunk back into the awesome miles of the Tonga Trench that waited hungrily beneath us.

I heard a sharp, metallic snap: It was Bob, a little better off than I, pulling the lever that opened the emergency escape kit.

The glow of the edenite film faded from the yellow-painted cylinder. The cap popped off. The plastic raft shot out of it, swelling out with a soft hiss of gas. . . .

Somehow we scrambled aboard. We got our helmets off and lay on our backs, getting back our strength.

The tall Pacific swell lifted us and dropped us, lifted us and dropped us. In the trough between the long, rounded waves we lay between walls of water; on the crest, we were hanging in midair in a plain of rolling black dunes. There were little sounds all around us—the wash of wavelets against the rubber raft, the sounds of the air, our own breathing, the little creaks and rattles the raft itself made.

It was utterly impossible to believe that four miles straight down a frightful battle was raging!

But Bob believed it; he remembered. Before I could get my breath back, before I could demand an explanation, he was up and about.

I lay there on the wet cushion of the raft, staring up at the blazing tropical stars that I had never expected to see again. My lungs and throat were burning still. I forced myself to sit up, to see what Bob was doing.

He was squatting at the end of the tiny raft, fussing over the sealed lockers that contained emergency rations, first aid medical equipment—and a radio-sonar distress transmitter.

It was the transmitter that Bob was frantically fumbling with.

"Bob!" I had to stop and cough. My throat was raw, sore, exhausted. "Bob, what's this all about? You've been acting so strangely——"

"Wait, Jim!"

I said: "I can't wait! Don't you realize that the Crakens and the rest of our friends down there may be dying by now? They needed us! Without our help the saurians are bound to break through——"

"Please, Jim. Trust me!"

Trust him! Yet there was nothing else I could do. I was cut off from the struggle at the bottom of Tonga Trench now as irrevocably as though it were being fought on the surface of the moon. It had taken perhaps ten minutes for us to get away from it—and it was literally impossible to get back. Even if there had been air for the pressure suit and power to keep its edenite shield going, what could I do? Cut loose and drop free? Yes—and land perhaps miles from the sea-mount where Jason Craken's besieged dome might even now be crumbling as the deeps pounded in. For I had no way of knowing what sub-sea currents had tossed us about as we came up—and would clutch at me again on the way down.

Trust him. It was a tall order—but somehow, I began to be able to do it.

I growled, "All right," and cleared my throat. Watching his fingers work so feverishly over the radio-sonar apparatus a thought struck me. I said: "One thing, anyway. When we get back to the Academy—if we ever do—I'll be able to report to Coach Blighman that you finally qualified . . at twenty thousand feet!"

He grinned briefly at me, and returned to the distress transmitter.

It was built to send an automatic SOS signal on distress frequency radio, and simultaneously on sonarphone. The sonarphone would reach any cruising subsea vessels within range—and precious short the range of a sonarphone was, of course. The radio component would transmit the same signal electronically. Of course, with most traffic under the surface of the sea these days, there would be few ships to receive it—but its range was thousands of miles, and somewhere there would be a ship, or a monitoring relay buoy re-transmitting via sonarphone to a subsea vessel beneath, to hear—and to act.

I bent closer to see what he was doing.

He was disconnecting the automatic signal tape!

While I watched, he completed his connections and switched on the transmitter. He picked up a tiny microphone on a short cable and began to talk into it.

I stared at him as I heard what he said.

"Diatom to radiolarian, diatom to radiolarian."

It didn't mean anything! It was the same garbled gibberish he had mumbled before. I had taken it to be the half-delirium of a mind just waking up from a shock—yet now he was saying it into a transmitter, and it was going out by radio and sonarphone to—to whom?

"Diatom to radiolarian," he said again, and again. "Diatom to radiolarian! The molluscans are ripe. Repeat, the molluscans are ripe! *Hurry, radiolarian!*"

I sank back, unbelieving, as the little emergency raft bobbed up and down, up and down in the swell.

Below us, our friends were fighting for their lives.

And up here on the surface, where we had fled—my friend Bob Eskow had gone mad as old Jason Craken himself.

But—appearances are deceiving.

I sat there on that wet, flimsy raft, staring at my friend. And finally I began to understand a few things.

Bob looked up at me, almost worriedly.

I said: "Hello, diatom."

He hesitated for a second, and then grinned. "So you've guessed."

"It took me long enough. But you're right, I've guessed. At least I think I have." I took a deep breath. "Diatom. That's your code name, right? You are diatom. And radiolarian—I suppose that's the code name for the Fleet? You're what we call an undercover agent, Bob. You're on a mission. All this time—you've been working for the Fleet itself. You came with us not for the fun of it, not to help me pay my family's debt to the Crakens —but because the Fleet gave you orders. Am I right?"

He nodded silently. "Close enough," he said after a moment.

It was hard to take in.

But—now that I had the key, things began to fall into place. All those mysterious absences of Bob's back at the Academy—the hours, the afternoons, when he disappeared and didn't tell me where he had gone, when I thought he had been practicing for the underwater tests— he had been reporting to Fleet. When he had hesitated before promising secrecy to David Craken—it had been because he had his duty to the Fleet, and couldn't promise until David so worded it that it didn't conflict.

And most important of all—when he had seemed to be deserting our friends down there beneath us, at the bottom of the Trench, it was because he had to come up here, to use the radio to report to the Fleet!

I said: "I think I owe you an apology, Bob. To tell the truth, I thought——"

He interrupted me. "It doesn't matter what you thought, Jim. I'm only sorry I couldn't tell you the truth before this. But my orders——"

It was my turn to interrupt. "Forget it! But—what happens next?"

He looked sober. "I hope we're in time! 'The molluscans are ripe'—that's our SOS. It means the battle is going on, way down there at the bottom, Jim. The Fleet is supposed to be standing by, monitoring the radio for this signal. Then they're supposed to come racing up and——"

His voice broke. He said in a different tone: "They're supposed to come down, pick us up, and take over in the Trench. You see, the Fleet knew something was up here—but they couldn't interfere, as long as there was no violence. But we've cut it pretty fine, Jim. Now that the violence has started—I only hope they get here before it's too late!"

I started to say, "I wish we could——"

I stopped in the middle of the wish, and forgot what it was I was going to wish for.

Something fast and faintly glowing was brightening the swells beneath us. I pointed. "Look, Bob!"

It was a faint blue shimmer in the black water; it grew brighter, and shaped itself into the long hull of a sub-sea ship, strangely familiar, surfacing close to us.

"They're here!" I cried. "Bob, they're here!"

He stared at the gleaming hull, then at me.

He said dazedly, "I should have cut off the sonarphone. They heard me."

"What are you talking about?" I demanded. "You wanted the Fleet, didn't you?"

I stopped then, because all at once I knew I was wrong—badly wrong, terribly wrong.

I knew then why that long hull, shimmering blue under the gentle wash of the waves, had seemed familiar. I hardly heard Bob saying:

"That's not the Fleet. It's the *Killer Whale!* They heard my message on the sonarphone!"

21

Aboard the Killer Whale

The amphibians had us aboard their sub-sea cruiser and hatches closed. I don't think it took more than a minute. We were too startled, too shocked to put up much of a fight.

And there was no point to a fight, not any more. If there was any hope for us anywhere, it was as likely to be aboard the *Killer* as waiting hopelessly on the raft.

The *Killer* stank. The fetid air reeked with the strange, sharp odor of the gleaming plants of the Trench, the aroma I associated with the amphibians. The whole ship was drenched with fog and trickling, condensed moisture. Everything we touched was wet, and clammy, and dappled with rust and mold.

There must have been twenty amphibians aboard the *Killer*. They manhandled us down the gangways, with hardly a word. I don't know if most of them spoke English or not; when they talked among themselves it was with such a slurring of the consonants and a singing of the vowels that I couldn't understand them.

But they took us to Joe Trencher.

The pearl-eyed leader of the amphibians was in the conn room, captain of the ship. He was naked to the waist and he had rigged up a spray nozzle on a water coupling that kept him continually drenched with salt water.

He stood scowling at us while he sprayed his fishbelly skin. He looked like some monster from an old legend, but I didn't miss the fact that he had conned the ship into a steep, circling dive as briskly as any Fleet officer.

"Why do you interfere against us?" he demanded.

I spoke for both of us. "The Crakens are our friends. And the Fleet has jurisdiction over the whole sea bottom."

He scowled without speaking for a moment. He broke into a fit of coughing and wheezing under his spray.

"I've caught a cold," he muttered accusingly, glowering at us. "I can't stand this dry air!"

Bob said sharply: "It isn't dry. In fact, you're ruining this ship! Don't you know this moisture will rot it out?"

Trencher said angrily: "It is my ship! Anyway——" he shrugged—"it will last long enough. Already we have defeated the Crakens and once they are gone we shall no longer need this ship."

I took a deep breath. Defeated the Crakens! I asked: "Are they—are they——"

He finished for me. "Dead, you mean?" He shrugged again. "If they are not, it will be only a short time. They are defeated, do you hear me?" He hurled the spray nozzle away from him as though the mere thought of them had infuriated him. At least there was still some hope, I thought. If they could only hold out a little longer. . . .

Trencher was wheezing: "Explain! We saw you flee to the surface, and we heard your message. But I do not understand it! Who is diatom? Who is radiolarian? What do you mean about the molluscans?"

Bob glanced at me, then moved a step toward him.

"I am diatom," he said. "Radiolarian is my superior officer, Trencher—a commander of the Sub-Sea Fleet! As diatom, I was on a special mission—concerning the Tonga pearls and you and your people. I needed information, and I got it; and my message will bring the whole Fleet here, if necessary, to put down any resistance and take over this entire area!" He sounded absolutely self-assured, absolutely confident. I hardly recognized him!

He went on, with a poise that an admiral might envy: "This is your last chance, Trencher. I advise you to give up. I'm willing to accept your surrender now!"

It was a brave attempt.

But the amphibian leader had courage of his own.

For a moment he was shaken; he stood there, blinking and wheezing, with a doubt in his eye. But then he exploded into raucous, gasping laughter. He caught up his spray again and wet himself down, still laughing.

"Ridiculous," he hissed, wheezing. "You are fantastic, young man. I have you here aboard my ship, and you live only as long as I wish to let you live. And you ask me to surrender!"

Bob said quickly: "It's your only chance. I——"

"Silence!" Trencher bellowed. He stood there, panting and scowling for a moment, while he made up his mind. "Enough. Perhaps you are a spy—I don't know. But I heard your message, and I did not hear a reply. Did it reach the Fleet? I think not, my young air-breather. And you will not have another chance, for we are now diving toward the Trench."

He played the spray nozzle on his face, staring at us through the tiny slits that half-covered his pearly eyes. "You will not see the sky again, young man. I cannot let you live."

Joe Trencher shrugged and spread his webbed fingers in a gesture that disclaimed responsibility. It was a sentence of death, and both Bob and I knew it.

Yet—even in that moment, I saw something in the amphibian's cold, pearly eyes that might almost have been sadness—compassion—regret.

He said heavily: "It is not that I wish to destroy you. It is only that you have left us no choice. We must keep the secret of the Tonga Trench to ourselves, and you wish to tell it to the world. We cannot allow that! We must keep you in the Trench. It is too bad that you cannot breathe salt water—but it is your misfortune, not ours, that this air will not last forever."

I was sweating, even in the cold and damp, but I tried to reason with him. "You can't keep your secret, Trencher. The exploration of the sea is moving too fast. If we don't come back, other men will be here to find the saurians and the shining weed and the Tonga pearls."

"They may come." He nodded heavily. "But we can't let them go back to the surface."

I demanded: "Why?"

"Because we are different, air-breather!" Trencher blinked, like a sad-faced idol in some queer temple, with Tonga pearls for eyes. "We learned our lesson many generations ago! We are mutations, as Jason Craken calls us—but once we were human. Our ancestors lived on the islands. And when some of us tried to go back, the islanders tried to kill us! They drove us into the sea. We found the Trench—and it is a kind world for us, young man, a world where we can live at peace.

"At peace—as long as we are left alone!"

He was wheezing and panting and struggling for breath—and it seemed to me that part of his distress was in his feelings and his mind. He sounded earnest and tragic. Even though he was saying that, in cold blood, he was going to take our lives—I couldn't help thinking that I almost understood how he felt.

Perhaps he had good reasons to hate and fear the breathers of air!

I said slowly: "Trencher, it seems there have been mistakes on both sides. But don't you see, we must make a peace that is fair to your people and to men! Men need you—but you need men, as well. You amphibians can be of great help in carrying out the conquest of the sea-bottoms. But our society has many things you must have as well. Medicine. Scientific discoveries. Help of a thousand kinds——"

"And more than that," Bob put in, "you need the protection of the Fleet!"

Trencher snorted, and paused to breathe his salt fog again.

"Jason Craken tried to tell us that," he puffed contemptuously. "He tried to bribe us with the trinkets your civilization has to offer—and when we welcomed him, he tried to turn us to slaves! The gifts he gave us were weapons to conquer us!"

"But Craken is insane, Trencher!" I told him. "Don't you see that? He has lived here alone so long that his mind is wandering; he needs medical care, attention. He needs to be placed in an institution where he can be helped. He needs a——"

"What he needs," Trencher wheezed brutally, "is a tomb. For I do not think he is any longer alive."

He paused again, thoughtfully, and once more it seemed there was a touch of regret in his milky eyes. "We thought he was our friend," he said, "and perhaps it is true that his mind has deserted him. But it is too late now. There were other men once, too—other men we thought our friends, and we could have trusted them. But it is also too late for that. It is too late for anything now, air-breathers, for as I left the dome to follow you to the surface it could have been only a matter of minutes until it fell."

I asked, on a sudden impulse: "These other men—what were their names?"

He glanced at me, wheezing, his opaque pearly eyes curious. "Why," he said, "they were——"

There was an excited, screaming cry from one of the other amphibians. I couldn't understand a word of it.

But Joe Trencher did! He dived for the microsonar screen the other amphibian had manned.

"The Fleet!" he wheezed, raging. "The Fleet!"

And it was true, for there in the screen were a dozen fat blips—undersea men-of-war, big ones, coming fast!

The *Killer Whale* went into a steep, twisting dive, and there was a rush and a commotion among its crew. Bob and I were manhandled, hurled aside, out of the way.

I felt the *Killer* shudder, and knew that jet missiles were streaking out toward the oncoming task force. We were in trouble now, no doubt about it! For if the Fleet won, it would be by blasting the *Killer* to atoms—and us with it; and if the Fleet, by any miraculous mischance should lose . . . then Joe Trencher would put us to breathing salt water, when the air ran out!

I said tensely to Bob: "At least they got your message! There's still some hope!"

He shrugged, eyes fast to the bank of microsonars. We were nearing the bottom of the Trench now. I could pick out the dimly seen shape of the sea-mount, the valleys and cliffs about it. I said, out of a vagrant thought, "I wish—I wish the Fleet hadn't turned up just then. I had an idea that——"

Bob looked at me "That what?"

I hesitated. "Well—that the men he spoke of were, well, someone we might know. But I couldn't hear the names——"

"You couldn't?" Bob asked, while the amphibians milled and shouted around us. "I could. And you're right, Jim—the men he said he might have been able to trust were the only other men who have ever been down here. Stewart Eden and your father!"

I stared at him.

"Bob! But—but don't you see? Then there's a chance! If he would trust them, then perhaps he'll listen to me! We've got to talk to him, stop this slaughter while there's still some hope—"

"Hope?"

Bob laughed sharply, but not with humor. He gestured at the microsonar screens, where the bottom of the Trench now was etched sharp and bright. "Take a look," he said in a tight, choked voice. "Take a look, and see what hope there is."

I looked.

Hope? No—not for the Crakens, at any rate; not for Laddy Angel, or Roger Fairfane, or the man who had saved my life once before, Gideon Park.

There was the sea-mount, standing tall in its valley; and there was the dome Jason Craken had built.

But it no longer stood high above the slope of the sea-mount.

The saurians had done their frightful work.

The edenite shield was down—barely a glimmer from a few scattered edges of raw metal.

And the dome itself—it was smashed flat, crushed, utterly destroyed.

22

"Panic is the Enemy!"

A dozen blossoming flares flashed in the microsonar screen at once.

It was the Fleet, replying to the *Killer's* fire. There was a burst of flares to starboard, a burst to port, a burst above.

Joe Trencher wheezed triumphantly: "Missed us!"

"That was no miss!" I rapped out. "We're bracketed, Trencher! That was a salvo from the Fleet unit to warn us to halt and cease offensive action—otherwise, the next salvo will be zeroed in on us!"

He choked and rasped: "Be quiet!" And he cried orders

148

to the other amphibians, in the language I could not understand.

The *Killer Whale* leaped and swung, and darted around behind the wreck of the dome, into the patterned caverns and fissures where the saurians maintained their breeding place. The *Killer* swooped into a crevice near what had once been the base of the dome itself; in the microsonar screen I could see the looming walls of the crevice closing in behind us and below. I thought I could see things moving back there—big things. Big as saurians. . . .

But at least the *Killer* was out of sight of the Fleet.

Gently it dropped to the rocky floor of the cut.

There was a sharp, incomprehensible order from Trencher, and the whir of the motors, the pulse of the pile-generators, stopped.

We lay there, waiting.

The chorus of ragged breathing from the amphibians grew louder, harsher. No one spoke.

All of us were watching the microsonar screens.

The Fleet was out of sight now—hidden behind the rimrock and the shattered remains of the dome.

The dome itself lay just before us. So short a time before, when Bob and I had raced up to give the warning, it had stood proud and huge, commanding the entrances to the breeding caves of the saurians. Now—wreckage. A few odd bits and pieces of metal stuck jaggedly above the ruin. Here and there was a section of a chamber, a few square yards of wall, that still seemed to keep a vestige of their original shape. Nothing else.

Joe Trencher had said that what the Crakens needed was a tomb. But this was their tomb, here before us—theirs, and the tomb of Roger and Laddy and my loyal, irreplaceable friend Gideon as well.

Joe Trencher broke into a ragged, violent fit of coughing.

I stared at him, watching closely.

Something was going on behind that broad, contorted face. There were traces of expression, moments of unguarded emotion—unless I missed my guess, the amphibian was beginning to regret what he had done—and to realize that there was no more hope for him than for us.

It was a moment when I might risk speaking.

I walked up to him. He glanced up, but not a man among the amphibians moved to stop me. I tried to read what was behind the glowing, pearly eyes; but it was hopeless.

I said: "Trencher, you said there were two other men you could trust. Were their names both—Eden?"

He scowled fiercely—but, I thought, without heart. "Eden? How do you know their names? Are they enemies too?"

I said: "Because my name is Eden too. One of those men was my father. The other—my uncle." Trencher scowled in surprise, and hid behind his spray of salt water. I pressed on: "You said you could trust them, Trencher. You were right. My father has passed away, but my uncle still lives—and it was because he helped me that I was able to come here. Won't you trust me? Let me talk to the Fleet commander on the sonarphone—see if we can work out truce terms?"

There was a long moment of silence, except for the wheezing and choking of the amphibians.

Then Joe Trencher put away his salt spray and looked at me. He said bleakly: "Too late!"

And he gestured at the microsonar screen, where the wreckage of Jason Craken's dome lay strewn before us.

Too late.

We all looked, and I knew what he meant. Certainly it was too late for anyone who was crushed in those ruins, under the weight of the sea. And in another sense, it was too late for Joe Trencher and his people—for they had certainly put themselves outside the pale of human law by causing those deaths.

But—something was out of key, in those ruins. Something didn't quite jibe.

I looked, and looked again.

One section of the ruins was intact. And—*it glowed with the foxfire of a working edenite shield.*

And from it was coming an irregular twinkling light. It was faint, reflected from some halfhidden viewport; but it was no illusion. It was there, blinking in a complicated code.

Complicated? Yes—for it was the code of the Sub-Sea Fleet; it was a distress call!

They were still alive!

Somehow, they had managed to get into one section of the dome where a functioning edenite shield had survived the destruction of the rest of the structure!

I said to Joe Trencher: "This is your chance, Trencher. They're still alive in there—now you can make your decision. Will you surrender to the Fleet?"

He hesitated.

I think he was about to agree.

But two things happened just then, that made his agreement to give up and submit to the laws of the Sub-Sea Fleet an academic matter.

There was a white rain of explosions patterning all over the microsonar screens—more than a dozen of them. The Fleet was moving in to destroy us!

And in the rear screen that peered down into the crevice in which we lay, something stirred and quivered and came racing toward us, huge and fast. One of the saurians was attacking!

That was a moment when time stopped.

We stood frozen, all of us, like chess pieces on a board, waiting for a player to make a move. Joe Trencher stared at the screen in a paralysis of indecision, and his amphibians waited on his signal. Bob and I—we watched. We watched, while the bright exploding fury of the Fleet's missiles churned the deeps into cream around us and the *Killer Whale* shook and quivered under the force of the surrounding explosions. We watched, while the giant, hurtling figure of the saurian came arrowing in upon us— closer and closer, looming huge and frightful in the sonar screen.

Frightful—and not alone! For on its back was a slim figure, bent low along the monstrous back, driving it forward with an elephant-goad.

It was the sea-girl, Maeva!

Joe Trencher's hand hovered over the firing control of his jet-missile gun.

I could not understand why he didn't shoot.

One of the amphibians screamed something in a shrill,

furious voice at Trencher—but Trencher only stared at the screen, his opaque pearly eyes filled with some emotion I could not read.

Crunch.

The speeding, raging figure of the saurian disappeared from the screen—and a moment later, the *Killer Whale* shook and vibrated as the plunging beast rammed us.

We all tumbled across the deck—it was that heavy a blow that the rampaging saurian had dealt the *Killer*. In the screen I caught a glimpse of the saurian bouncing away, wildly struggling to regain its balance, beating the water with its clumsy-seeming oars of limbs. It had been hurt—but it was still going, and its rider, the sea-girl, still had kept her seat. It had been hurt—but so were we.

The Troyon tube lights flickered, dimmed, and brightened again. Ominous warning! For if the power went— our edenite shield would go as well.

The amphibians were silent no longer. There was a chattering and screaming from them like a cage of madened monkeys. One of them was scrambling across the tilted deck toward the missile-gun controls. Joe Trencher picked himself up and made a dive for the other amphibian. But Trencher was groggy, slow—he had been hurt; the other pearly-eyed man turned to face him; they struggled for a second, and Trencher went flying.

The amphibian at the gun spun the controls as, in the screen, Maeva and her strange mount came plunging in for another attack.

There was scarcely time to think, in that moment of wild strife and confusion. But—Bob and I were cadets of the Sub-Sea Academy and we had learned, what generations of cadets before us had learned so well, that there is *always* time to think. "Panic is the enemy!" That motto is dinned into us, from the moment we arrive as lubbers until Graduation Day.

Never panic.

Think—then act!

I whispered to Bob: "It's time for us to take a hand!"

Trencher and the other amphibian were locked in a struggle over the controls of the missile-gun; one shot had been fired, and it seemed Trencher was trying to prevent

152

another. The remaining amphibians, half a dozen of them or more, were milling about in a state of confusion.

We hit them full amidships, with everything we had. It was a fierce, bloody struggle for a moment. But they were confused and we were not; we knew what we had to do. Some of them wore sidearms; we hit them first, and got their guns before the others could come to their senses.

And the fight was over almost before it got started. Bob and I had the guns.

We were masters of the *Killer Whale!*

We stood there, breathing hard, guns drawn and leveled.

Joe Trencher cast one bright, maddened look at the microsonar screen and came toward us.

"Hold it!" I yelled. "I'll——"

"No, no!" he cried. He skidded to a halt, gestured at the screen. "I want—I only want to go out there. To help Maeva! Don't you see?"

I risked a glance at the screen.

It was true—she needed help. That one wild shot from the missile gun had struck her mount, Old Ironsides. It was beating the water to froth—aimlessly, agonizedly. The girl herself was gone from its back—stunned by the gun, perhaps, if not worse. Even as we watched, the monster began to weaken. It turned slowly over and over, beginning to sink. . . .

Bob whispered: "It may be a trick! Can we trust him?"

I looked at Joe Trencher, and I made my decision. "Go ahead!" I ordered. "See if you can help her—we owe her that!"

The opaque eyes glanced at me for only a second; then Joe Trencher flashed past me, toward the lock.

He paused, while the inner door of the lock was opening. He gasped: "You've won, air-breather." He hesitated. "I—I'm glad you won."

And then he was gone. In a moment we heard the thud of water coming into the lock.

I ordered: "Bob! Get on the sonarphone to the Fleet. Tell them to hold their fire. It's all over—we've won!"

And that was the end of the adventure of the Tonga Trench.

We found our friends, in that little sealed cubicle that was all that was left of Jason Craken's castle beneath the sea. They were battered and weary—but they were alive. The sea-medics of the Fleet came in and took charge of them. It was easy enough to heal the bruises and scars of Gideon and Roger and Laddy and David Craken. When it came to old Jason, the medics could do little. It was not the flesh that was sick, it was the mind. They took him away as gently as they could.

He didn't object. In his clouded brain, he was still the emperor of the Tonga Trench, and they were his subjects.

Maeva came to see us off. She held David's hand and turned to me. "Thank you," she said, "for giving Joe Trencher his chance to save me. If he hadn't come to get me——"

I shook my head. "You deserve all the thanks that are going," I told her. "If it hadn't been for you and Old Faithful ramming us just then, Bob and I never would have been able to take over the *Killer Whale*. And Trencher himself helped. He wouldn't let the other amphibians shoot you—I don't know why."

She looked at me, astonished. She and David turned to each other, and then David looked back at me and smiled.

"You didn't know?" he asked. "It isn't surprising that Joe wouldn't let them shoot Maeva . . . since she is, after all, his daughter. . . ."

The last we saw of Maeva she was swimming beside the ship that bore David and Bob and me, waving farewell to the microsonar scanners.

All about us in the screens were the long, bright silhouettes of men-of-war of the Sub-Sea Fleet, returning to station after ending the struggle of the Tonga Trench. She looked oddly tiny and alone against the background of those dreadnaughts of the deep.

She could not see us, but we waved back. "Good-by," said Bob, under his breath.

But David slapped him on the back and grinned. "Don't say 'good-by,'" he ordered. "Say '*au revoir.*' We're coming back!"